Knotty Girl
By Maggie Casper

Roping the naughty girl is all fun and games until someone falls in love.

Shelby Langley was not sub, slave or Mistress, she was merely kinky. Point her to a BDSM club where she could watch and experience pretty much anything the mind could conjure, without the tangled web of an actual relationship, and she was in orgasmic bliss.

Long into the lifestyle, Craig Jensen was able to spot a submissive in denial from a mile away. Usually he left them be to find their own way, only keeping an eye out for their safety while on his turf, but there was something about the sweet, young blonde who had a love for rope bondage that called for him to claim her as his own.

Warning, this title contains the following: explicit sex, graphic language, anal play and an overall spanking good time.

Ladies! Meet Red Hot Alaskan Men
By Nancy Lindquist

Chastity Cuthbert is determined to bring love and romance to the Last Frontier.

Chastity Cuthbert is in love with love. Its too bad that she's so busy working on everyone else's happily ever after that there's no time left to work on hers. Her company, The Alaskan Connection, matches single women with sexy Alaskan hunks. Business is booming. Until Dave Wellington drags his personal vendetta against outsiders right to her doorstep.

Dave Wellington, Mayor of Smithfield, Alaska won't allow Chastity's cadre of red-lipped floozies to take over his town. A she-bitch from the lower forty-eight broke his brother's heart and no one else is gonna go through that. Not if he can help it. Besides, Smithfield is welcoming tourists for the first time. The male residents need to keep their minds on business. Not sex.

Determined to change Chastity's mind, he travels to Chicago to talk her out of her plan. Chas is so pissed off at the sexy mayor that she forgets her "no one-night stands" motto. Right into Dave's bed.

Now she has to travel to Smithfield and face him. She's strong. She can face Dave again. Just because she snuck out of his hotel room in the middle of the night doesn't mean she's a big ole chicken. Right?

Skin to Skin

By Dionne Galace

What Leilani wants, Leilani gets...and she always gets her man.

What Leilani wants, Leilani gets. That is, until she meets the enigmatic Oliver Clayton, her new neighbor. For some reason, Oliver seems to be intent on avoiding her even though he's obviously interested. Leilani has tried to everything to get his attention, from wearing skimpy little outfits to walking a neighbor's dog six times in front of his yard. Leilani wants Oliver...and she always gets her man.

In the heat of the summer, the temperature's not only thing rising. Luckily, Oliver has that pool in his backyard and Leilani knows just how to cool off...

Warning, this title contains the following: explicit sex, graphic language, light bondage.

Sealed With a Kiss
By Lila Dubois

When a man who isn't human is accidentally enslaved by a woman who has no idea what he is, the result is magical.

Signing up for a one-week adventure vacation, Helena expects to be kayaking in the Pacific, not having every sexual fantasy fulfilled in her guide's bed.

Ocean is more than he seems, his kayaking business a cover for his deepest secret.

When Helena accidentally enacts old magic, enslaving Ocean, he doesn't know if she is the luckiest girl on earth, or an enemy of his kind, bent on imprisoning him forever. Ocean's strange behavior worries Helena but she's distracted by the mind-blowing sex.

After the truth is revealed, will their budding love be Sealed with a Kiss?

Warning, this title contains the following: explicit sex, graphic language, voyeurism, and fantasy fulfillment.

Overheated

A Samhain Publishing, Ltd. publication.

Samhain Publishing, Ltd.
577 Mulberry Street, Suite 1520
Macon, GA 31201
www.samhainpublishing.com

Knotty Girl, 1-59998-583-7
First Samhain Publishing, Ltd. electronic publication: August 2007
Ladies! Meet Red Hot Alaskan Men, 1-59998-585-3
First Samhain Publishing, Ltd. electronic publication: July 2007
Skin to Skin, 1-59998-589-6
First Samhain Publishing, Ltd. electronic publication: August 2007
Sealed With a Kiss, 1-59998-593-4
First Samhain Publishing, Ltd. electronic publication: August 2007
First Samhain Publishing, Ltd. print publication: June 2008

Contents

Knotty Girl

Maggie Casper

~9~

Ladies! Meet Red Hot Alaskan Men

Nancy Lindquist

~69~

Skin to Skin

Dionne Galace

~141~

Sealed With a Kiss

Lila Dubois

~197~

Knotty Girl

Maggie Casper

Dedication

To MG for explaining to me exactly what it is a Pro Top does.

Chapter One

"I think I'd better stick with rope."

Craig Jensen wanted to shake some sense into the petite naked blonde who lay shivering at his feet. Even clouded with confusion after her dead faint, her eyes were the greenest he'd ever seen. And her curves may very well be wearing curves all their own but neither attribute changed the fact that she was reckless on top of being trouble with a capital T.

"I mean, geez, whoda thought plastic wrap could be so dangerous," she continued as if the scowl plastered across his face made no difference in the world. That was amazing all on its own considering his scowl had the ability to scare grown men.

"Nope, I'll stick with rope. After all, it doesn't make me sweat and feels so damn good against my skin that just the thought of it makes me..."

She stopped mid-sentence as if she'd just realized what she was saying. Color returned to her cheeks as her gaze settled on his.

"You little fool." His words were low and heated as he draped a robe over her prone body.

The rest of the crowd had dispersed, leaving only himself, the blonde and the idiot young dominant she'd been playing with. Grabbing the rather large ball of plastic wrap that had been used to bind her, in effect mummifying her from shoulder to ankle, he stood to his full height of six feet, two inches.

Without taking his gaze from his patient, Craig handed the ball of plastic wrap to the deathly pale man standing beside him. "She's going to be fine."

The skinny punk sighed in relief. Feeling a bit of compassion for the young man, Craig said, "Accidents are bound to happen in this lifestyle, especially for a new dom. Take this as a lesson and learn from it, but don't let anything like it happen here again. Ever."

His words were clipped and deadly serious. The young man listening intently evidently knew Craig meant business because his demeanor changed from that of rebellion to keen interest. It wouldn't be long before the new dom was all but begging for lessons.

Craig had already been there, done that as a Pro Top. For years he'd received payment for services rendered. At one time he'd had several dominant-submissive couples who he tutored and many singles who either wanted to learn a particular aspect such as wielding a flogger or experience the receiving end. He had no intention of doing it again.

Other than overseeing Club Jerico, the BDSM club he'd built from the ground up then sold, lock, stock and barrel to his best friend, Craig now had the time he needed to look for his one, the one submissive in a long line of women who would truly be his. Wasn't it ironic that out of all the experienced women he'd played with over the years, the obviously inexperienced blonde still at his feet was the one? Hell, he didn't even know her name.

It was crazy. Craig couldn't explain how he knew she was the one. It was just something he was certain of. Something he felt bone deep. He'd seen and played with hundreds of women over the years but something about the one at his feet was different.

She was everything he normally stayed away from in a play partner. So why in the hell did he feel as though life as he knew it would never be the same if he didn't own her, heart, body and soul?

"Oh, and she's off limits. Make it known."

The young man's head swung from where she now sat on the floor back to him before he nodded and left. Craig couldn't help but smile.

"What the hell is wrong with you, mister?"

Yep, she was a firecracker all right. Craig watched as she struggled to her feet on wobbly legs, all the while trying to keep her nude flesh covered. The last was something Craig found funny considering not more than a half hour before she'd been completely nude, with nothing more than a thin layer of plastic wrap over her. She was going to be hell to tame but if his gut instinct was correct, she'd be worth every single second of the long journey ahead.

Craig shook his head. He didn't believe in love at first sight—lust maybe. So why then was his heart pounding like he'd just run a marathon? And why in the world did the thought of her helpless and possibly injured make him feel ill?

"You play with an unknown, doing something that leaves you as helpless as mummification without knowing the possible dangers then pass out cold and you want to know what the hell is wrong with me." He couldn't believe the audacity of the little imp. "What's your name, girl?"

"I'm not a girl, I'm a woman, and why do you want to know?" Huffed out all in one breath, her comeback was quick and full of attitude.

Craig moved across the room, smiling secretly when she followed. She needed some water and a place to sit, even if she didn't know it. He reached into one of the ice chests providing drinks for the patrons of the club and extracted a bottle of water for her.

"Either you tell me your name or I'll continue to call you girl. Your decision."

Offering choices was a good thing, especially early on. It always gave some semblance of control to the one doing the choosing. And until the little spitfire shooting daggers at him from her eyes came to the conclusion that she was submissive, more importantly, his submissive, Craig would have to go slow.

If there was one thing he'd learned over the years it was that submission not freely given was not submission at all. And God only knew that every fiber of his being wanted her submission and so much more.

"I must have missed the memo stating I now have a keeper. Sheesh."

Oh hell no, she just didn't. The woman, and Craig used that term loosely considering how young and inexperienced she obviously was, didn't know when to quit. "What was that?"

She wrinkled her nose and muttered, "Nothing."

Of course, there was always the chance he was wrong in thinking she was submissive. It had been known to happen, Craig smirked to himself, thinking back on some of the whack jobs he'd gotten himself involved with. Older, and hopefully wiser, he decided to learn as much as possible about her before coming to any conclusions. Now if only he could get his cock to agree.

With a hand on her arm just above her elbow, Craig led them to a dimly lit quiet corner. Once they were both seated, he handed her the bottle of water and nudged her to drink.

"You're probably just a bit dehydrated. Combine that with sweating in plastic wrap for a prolonged amount of time and an overdose of sexual energy and it will almost always equal disaster."

He waited through a few minutes of silence before repeating his earlier question. "What's your name?"

"Shelby."

Her single-word answer was clipped and accompanied by the most amusing look of irritation he'd ever seen on such a pixie-like face.

"So, Shelby, how did you come to learn about Club Jerico?"

She peered up at him from beneath long lashes. Craig couldn't remember the last time he'd seen a grown woman appear so innocent.

"Word of mouth." Her answer was obviously reluctant. She acted as though being in his presence was the last place she wanted to be.

"Are you new to town?"

Shelby twisted the cap back on her bottle of water before speaking. "I was born and raised here."

That came as a complete shock to Craig. He may not be an outgoing person where the vanilla community was concerned, but she was at a BDSM club and for the most part, he knew pretty much everyone involved in the lifestyle for miles around. Or so he'd thought.

"New to the lifestyle then or just experimenting? I haven't seen you around."

She huffed out a breath then proceeded to twist a lock of curly blonde hair around her finger in an action Craig wasn't sure whether to consider seductive, childish, nervous, or very possibly a combination of the three.

"My folks own Langley's Launch out on the lake. I've been away at school but came home for summer break to help out."

Now they were getting somewhere. Shelby Langley. Craig had heard about her, knew the name just as anyone who spent any time at all at the lake would. Her parents owned and operated the only docking area, boat fueling station and restaurant to service the large body of water.

The thought of her leaving after summer was over bothered him. Would there be enough time to claim her for his own? And if not, would he be able to let her go? The thought actually made Craig's chest ache, which irritated him to no end. Was he turning into a sap? Hell, he'd barely met her, there was no way he could already be falling for her on more than a purely sexual level. Was there?

Craig shook the thought from his head. Many things needed to happen before he should even worry about her leaving, like getting her to understand she belonged to him and no one else.

The wickedly twisted side of him could hardly wait for the fun to begin.

Shelby looked at the man sitting next to her. He was big, much larger than her own five-foot stature, and the kind of sexy that would have soaked her panties in seconds had she been wearing any.

He was clearly dominant and not in the I-can-be-top-now-and-bottom-later way she preferred in the men she played with. This man would want, no he would *insist* on owning. He would claim and never release.

The truth was evident in the intensity of his brown-eyed gaze, and it affected Shelby in ways that made her uncomfortable in her own skin.

"What's your name? I mean, you know just about everything there is to know about me but I know next to nothing about you. I don't even—"

"Craig. Craig Jensen. I run this place."

The way he cut her off made Shelby wonder if her penchant for talking irritated him. If it did, well that was just too damn bad. As a matter of fact, she'd just have to file that little tidbit away for future use. Could come in handy.

"Well, it was nice to meet you, Craig Jensen." Shelby stood, her legs finally feeling more normal and less rubber-like. "Thank you for your help. I'm sure I'll see you around sometime."

She took a step back and nearly sighed in relief when he didn't move. The look on his face was granite hard. He didn't appear too happy for some reason, a reason Shelby was sure she didn't need to know although her blasted curiosity almost had her blurting out what would surely be a stupid question.

Turning, she moved slowly across the room. It was rather comical to think about, but Shelby felt like prey trying not to garner the attention of a predator.

Her relief was short-lived when, after changing from the borrowed robe to her street clothes, she came out of the ladies room to find Craig waiting for her.

Shelby tried her best to pay him no attention. It was rude, something her mother would be displeased to know, but there was just something about the man following her that made Shelby uneasy in a way she'd never before experienced.

Ignoring a man such as Craig Jensen, with his shaved head and neatly trimmed goatee, was hard enough. Add to that a body so sexy her nipples couldn't help but stand up and take notice and the fact that he was so close made it nearly impossible.

Irritated not only by the heat pooling between her thighs but his presence, Shelby stopped dead in her tracks and turned to face him.

"Is there any special reason why you're following me, or do you see everyone to the door?"

She knew she was being a bitch but she did not want this man around her. Something about his closeness, the way he held himself, controlled himself, warned Shelby just how easily he could also control her if she gave him half the chance. And that was simply something she had no desire to do.

Oh, she didn't have any nasty secrets in her past. No psycho ex-Master or abusive boyfriend. Nope, Shelby was merely having fun by her kinky self and felt no need to change things.

"I'm driving you home."

His words pulled her back to the present like a splash of cold water to the face.

"That's not necessary, but thanks anyway." Shelby tried to keep her smile sweet and yet let him know she felt strongly about her decision to drive herself home. To show weakness to someone like the man standing before her would be a mistake of colossal proportions.

"I insist."

"You would." Shelby spoke the words like a challenge. Evidently being nice did not work. If blunt was what it took to get him to back off, then blunt was what he was going to get. "Look. I appreciate your offer but I am perfectly capable of getting myself home." There, that should get him off her back. She turned on her heel only to be stopped by Craig's hand on her arm.

"I'm sure you are more than capable, but that doesn't change anything. I'm driving you home." He tugged slightly on

18

Knotty Girl

her arm when she opened her mouth to argue. "You can either give me your keys and get in of your own free will or I'll carry you to my car and after I paddle your ass, I'll place you inside and drive you home. The choice is yours."

"Some choice." Shelby stalked the rest of the way to her car, equal amounts of anger and arousal coursing through her veins. There was something very twisted about her that she could in any way shape or form be aroused by such blatant highhandedness.

When they reached her car, she thrust the keys into Craig's hand. "How do you plan on getting back here?"

"I'll call a cab once we're on our way. It'll meet me at the lake." His answer made Shelby want to scream. He'd thought of everything.

The ride to the lake, although not long, seemed to take forever. Being quiet was a rare thing for Shelby so giving Craig the silent treatment was rough. In order to not ask questions, rant, rave or speak in pretty much any capacity, she had to close her eyes and concentrate.

Of course, not talking made her feel even antsier. Without thought to what she was doing, Shelby fidgeted with the zipper on her purse, unzipping and re-zipping it over and over until one of Craig's large hands closed over hers.

His touch was warm and solid, stopping her mid-zip. Shelby didn't want to like his touch. She didn't want the heat of his skin to arrow straight to her core and she sure the hell didn't want his closeness to make her wet, but it did all that and more.

It was the more part she was worried about. Something about him made her insides quiver and her heart pound. She'd come home to help out and have some fun, not to fall for the first dominant who seemed to have a clue what he was doing.

19

She wondered if his touch was planned. Could it have been more than just the need to stop her fidgeting? Did he know how his touch affected her? Just the thought had her narrowing her eyes at him across the dark interior of her car.

What he hadn't considered was that Shelby Langley was not some doormat submissive who he could point and snap his fingers at. She had a mind of her own and more opinions than most. If he thought her weak or easy to manage, he had another think coming.

Chapter Two

The wait was going to kill him. Of that, Craig was sure. Nearly a week had passed without seeing Shelby. She hadn't bothered to show up for the Wednesday night lifestyle group meeting and lecture on safety and BDSM, something that would have been beneficial for her given where her last experience had led her.

Instead, she'd stayed away and it was driving Craig insane. That alone had the ability to put him in a foul mood. He didn't stomp or lose his temper. As a dom and a leader in the local kink community, he was known for his iron control. So why did she have the ability to keep him so far on edge he couldn't wait to tumble over? It was sickening and pissed him off.

When a knock came at his closed door, he barked, "Come in!"

Sierra, one of his best waitresses, popped her head in, a knowing smile on her face. "I believe the little one you've been waiting for has finally showed up, Sir."

Craig chose to ignore the flash of humor in Sierra's eyes. He had more on his mind than sassy waitresses. He had important things to move on to, things that were sure to get very interesting, very soon if Shelby's reaction to him at their first meeting was any indication.

She may have tried her best to appear strong and in control around him but it had been hard to miss the hitch in her breathing at even the simplest touch from his hand.

Would she like it when he kissed her, taking her mouth with his lips, tasting her with his tongue? He could hardly wait to find out. If she enjoyed that she would surely enjoy the other things he had planned for her. Things like gliding his tongue over every inch of her bare flesh before finally settling on her heated core.

Once there he planned to work Shelby's body slowly, methodically. He would bring her to peak over and over without ever letting her tumble to her fulfillment. Then, just about the time she reached once again for her release, he would do something sinister like land a stinging swat to her inner thigh. Or perhaps he would merely stop his ministrations, leaving Shelby gasping for air and begging for more.

With a wicked smile curving his lips, Craig left his office in search of Shelby before she managed to get herself in trouble.

He made his way through the cavernous main room. It took a minute to spot Shelby in the far corner speaking with one of the regulars, a male submissive who had a foot fetish. He was eyeing her stiletto-heeled boots like they were a T-bone steak and he was a starving man.

That in and of itself was a comical sight, but the conversation he eavesdropped on as he stood just a few feet away was so damn funny he had trouble not laughing out loud.

"But I am sure you would make a wonderful domme, Miss Shelby."

She huffed an exasperated sigh. "I've told you before, I am not dom or sub. I just like to play. Besides..." her voice raised an octave, her agitation apparent, "...either my pits stink or something else I've done has offended because not one person will play with me tonight."

Just then she caught sight of him and visibly stiffened. The man she was talking to turned to see what had stopped their conversation.

Craig leveled the man with a look that spoke volumes. Within seconds, he was off but not before saying to Shelby, "If you're wondering about the no-play thing, you might want to ask him."

Before he made it to her, Shelby had her hands fisted on the curve of her hips, a booted toe tapping with impatience. "You didn't really mean it last time when you said I was off limits, did you?"

"Yes, I did."

Craig made it a habit to never lie and he had no intention of starting now. He also knew better than to pull the caveman routine with someone who didn't yet realize she belonged to him. Instead, he decided to take a more professional stance on the matter.

"You like to play, that much I can tell, but you are either inexperienced or careless. The latter concerns me, so if you want to play at Club Jerico you'll have to take me as your partner until I'm convinced you can handle the situations you might find yourself in."

Not used to explaining himself or his actions, Craig took a deep, fortifying breath. A storm brewed in Shelby's green eyes. Eyes that were narrowed in anger, causing her cheeks to flush.

It didn't take long for all of Craig's thoughts to travel south of his belt buckle, right along with the blood that had at one time occupied the rest of his body but now sat heavily in the thick length of his engorged cock.

He wanted to see her cheeks flush from the things he was going to do to her, his hands stroking her flesh, parting her folds for the exploration of his fingers.

One thought cascaded into another and before Craig knew what had hit him, he was in an all-out, lust-filled daydream consisting of Shelby with a red-hot, hand-printed ass. Her nipples would be engorged beneath clamps as he artfully wrapped her body in the finest hemp rope he could find.

"You can't be serious?" Shelby whispered the words as if she were afraid someone else might hear and be scandalized by his terms, tearing Craig from his thoughts. He had to concentrate on not laughing. The woman was just too much.

"I never say things I don't mean, Shelby." He looked deep into her wide-eyed gaze, holding her captive for a fraction of a second before punctuating exactly how serious he was. "Those are the terms of your continued play here. Take it or leave it."

Craig was unsure what he'd do if she walked. He'd end up going after her; that much he knew. He just wasn't sure exactly how much time he'd give her before showing up on her doorstep to claim what he already saw as his.

Things would be so much easier if, to begin with, she would agree with his terms and get to know him in a more playful, less permanent way.

She stared at him, mumbling beneath her breath. Craig couldn't quite make out the words rolling through her mind and across her luscious lips.

Then, as if she didn't have a care in the world, Shelby shrugged her bare shoulders. "I'll take it. Let's play."

Her words damn near brought Craig to his knees. Carefree and playful she might sound, but he knew better. Somewhere deep inside she was not only intrigued by what he had to offer but afraid of it as well.

First things first. "During the time you play here, you're mine." He held up a hand to ward off the coming argument. "I'm not finished."

When he was sure he had her complete attention, Craig continued. "I don't bottom. Ever. So plan on getting well acquainted with your submissive side."

The look on Shelby's face was priceless. Her nose wrinkled and her brow furrowed. Her cheeks were so red, Craig thought she might very well explode, but to her credit, she remained quiet.

"You'll have a safe word and every scene we take part in will be negotiated."

He looked her up and down in blatant perusal of her attributes. The denim shorts she wore didn't quite cover all of her ass and the strapless top did more than hint at cleavage, making his mouth water. She looked exactly like what she was, a young woman home from college for summer vacation. And she was all his.

When she opened her mouth, Craig interrupted, "Oh, and I don't share what is mine, even if only for a while, so don't plan on inviting anyone else along for the ride."

Out of every imaginable thing Craig thought Shelby might say in response to his drawn-out plan, the words to leave her mouth were not among them.

"Sounds good. Your rope or mine?"

Shelby couldn't help but smile at the look on Craig's face. His plan to protect her from herself, or whatever it was he was attempting to do, was a crock of shit as far as she was concerned. Like most of the other men she'd come across, dominant or not, he was more than likely just looking for a toy, someone to get him off. Shelby had no problem being that one as long as she got hers in the process.

Although, something about him warned that if she were smart, she'd head out the door and never look back. The way Craig made her feel when they were together warned it would be nearly impossible to keep her heart out of the equation.

But then again, when it came to her kinky side, being smart was the last thing on her mind. Not when standing right in front of her was a man so sexy he could make her wet with no more than the sound of his voice.

Who cares if he just wants a toy to play with, Shelby thought, trying in vain to ignore the tiny little voice in the back of her head insisting she did mind. She couldn't care, wouldn't allow herself to.

You're just here for the kink. Shelby repeated the mantra over and over in her head.

She couldn't wait to feel his lips on hers. Taking with a heat so all-fire consuming everything to follow would pale in comparison. Damn how she hoped that one day she'd find a man who knew how to kiss, really kiss, and loved doing it. Until then she'd bide her time testing her limits and finding out what her likes and dislikes were as far as being a kinkster.

Shelby looked up at Craig. He was so tall and wide-shouldered her mouth watered just thinking about the naughty things he could do to her with little to no effort.

There were walls to be pressed against, her feet dangling high above the floor, as well as desks to be placed over. So many delicious things came to mind she could hardly keep herself from purring out loud.

On the other hand, dropping to her knees, taking him in her mouth and blowing his mind also ranked pretty high on her want-to-do list.

Damn, something about the beast of a man kept Shelby not only irritated as hell but dripping wet and ready for sex.

Like any man used to being in control, Craig recovered very quickly.

"So, you like rope, do you?"

His voice was velvety smooth. It flowed over Shelby, causing her nipples to peak before the heat of her arousal pooled between her thighs. The sensations increased her awareness of how close their bodies were.

"Hell yeah." Being flippant was about the only way Shelby could think to lessen just how disturbing his proximity to her was.

The look in Craig's eyes spoke volumes. Only in her lust-induced stupor, Shelby was clueless as to what they were saying.

"Good, because I just happen to be pretty handy with a length of rope."

Shelby felt the blush rise in her cheeks. Trying to play it off, she allowed her lips to curve in what she was sure was a killer, let's-play smile.

Evidently playing the seductive vamp didn't work on someone of Craig's caliber...or was it maturity? Once again, she was clueless.

"Good. Follow me then."

"Lead the way."

This time her flippant remark stopped him dead in his tracks. "Any time we're together in a lifestyle capacity, you'll refer to me as Sir."

He moved to cross the room without ever looking back to see whether she was there or not, which irritated Shelby to no end. Acting on impulse, she did the first thing that came to mind.

With a click of her heels and a mock salute, Shelby spoke in a voice full of attitude. "Aye, aye, Captain, *Sir*."

Once finished acting like a fool, she followed Craig. Shelby was sure she was going to pay for her behavior and was kicking her own ass because of it. Would she ever learn?

"Probably not in this lifetime," she mumbled to herself before moving across the threshold of a room outfitted with nothing more than a very large four-poster bed.

Oh yes!

Shelby all but rubbed her hands together in glee. She wasn't really one to jump into bed with just anybody no matter what it seemed like to the outside world, but damn, it had been a long dry spell. At the ripe young age of twenty-five, she was due and would take all she could get.

"First things first." Craig's voice pulled her gaze from the surface of the overly large bed. "Unless you've got a safe word you prefer to use, we'll do it the easy way and stick with yellow and red."

It sounded like a good plan to Shelby, who merely nodded her agreement. There was just something about that bed, which sat in a room in a house filled with all types of kinky people, that had her adrenaline pumping in a purely exhibitionist sort of way.

"Do you understand, Shelby?"

Geez, what did he think she was, five? "Yeah, I understand."

His brow furrowed. "Yeah?"

It took Shelby a minute to get where he was going. She'd always sworn to herself she'd never use a title when referring to a play partner. But as with anything else in life, never was a long time. For some off-the-wall reason, it didn't seem so awful to bestow the title upon Craig. Of course, that bit of information was something she didn't want to think about just yet.

"Yes, Sir. I understand. Red means stop and yellow means I need you to slow down."

His smile was warm and reached his whiskey brown eyes, crinkling the corners in a way that melted a little section of her heart.

"Good girl." It was absolutely mind-boggling to Shelby why words that should have raised her ire instead gave her a secret thrill.

They spent a few minutes going over her experiences and what she considered to be her hard limits, or the things she wouldn't consider doing no matter what, before proceeding.

"Okay then, do you have anything on under those?" Craig motioned toward her cut-off shorts.

"Panties."

Shelby wasn't at all sure where he was going with his line of questioning. She might not have the perfect body, but she knew she was sexy as hell and had no trouble flaunting what she did have.

From what she could tell, most men would rather have a real woman—scars, stretch marks and all—who was confident in her own skin, over a Barbie doll who was afraid of a full meal.

"Leave them on, but everything else has to go." Craig turned back to the door, locking it. Evidently he wasn't much for public play. Things were about to get interesting, Shelby thought as she slowly lowered her strapless top below the generous swell of her breasts before shimmying it over her hips.

When the garment was completely free of her body, she folded it and laid it over the back of a close-by chair then began working on the snap of her shorts. Within seconds Shelby was nude except for the barely there triangle of her fire engine red g-string.

"Mmm, very nice."

She was a bit surprised by his praise. The warmth in his voiced compliment shouldn't matter, but it did.

"Thank you, Sir." This time around, adding the title seemed almost natural. She was dumbfounded by the unexplainable need to please him, to see his smile once again.

When he pulled a length of rope from a small bag Shelby hadn't even noticed, her heart rate skyrocketed. He moved toward her at a leisurely pace, slowly pulling the length of rope through his hand. The look in his eyes was intense, full of heat and arousal that called to every fiber of her being.

Craig Jensen was dangerous to her peace of mind and yet, Shelby couldn't seem to care.

Chapter Three

He started by ever so slowly wrapping the rope around Shelby's chest just above her breasts and then again just below. It didn't take long before Shelby relaxed into the hug of rope, her eyes glazed.

She was glorious in her arousal. Absolutely, stunningly beautiful. He was falling hard and fast, something that completely boggled his mind considering he'd yet to ever find himself in the same predicament with any woman, much less one he'd just met.

Craig decided to up the ante a bit. He added to the chest harness of rope in a way that would heighten her arousal by bringing her nipples into play.

This time the length of doubled rope was passed over the peaked tips then separated before being pulled tight and secured, in effect forming a built-in set of clamps.

From their earlier conversation, Craig knew rope play had the ability to make Shelby extremely aroused, possibly even sending her into subspace. Not wanting to interrupt the sensations flowing over her, Craig spoke low and soft.

"On your back on the bed, little one." He put actions to words by helping her get into position.

Once there he used the chest harness with the addition of two other lengths of rope to secure her to the headboard of the bed. Another two lengths of rope cuffed her ankles, securing them to the footboard, in effect leaving her helpless, except for her free hands.

As much as Craig loved physical bondage—the sight of a woman bound and at his whim—the real thrill of power exchange, at least for him, came from the mental aspects.

Anyone could tie a person up, but to bind merely with words added a whole new dimension to the scene, and that was exactly what he had planned for Shelby.

Her pretty green eyes were closed, her breath coming in deep draws that expanded her lungs, inflicting the will of the rope upon her nipples in a way that made his cock rock hard with desire.

"Shelby. I want you to place your arms above your head, palms on the headboard, and leave them there until I tell you otherwise. Do you understand?"

Why he'd insisted she call him sir when he'd never instructed a submissive, not even his own, to bestow a title upon him, Craig had no idea. Not knowing didn't stop him from doing it. It also didn't stop him from asking questions just to hear her say that word.

Her breathy *Yes, Sir* stirred something inside of Craig he hadn't felt for quite some time, if ever. The next part of his plan could very well backfire if he'd pegged Shelby all wrong.

"Look at me."

He kept his words low yet firm. Shelby responded immediately, her lashes fluttering against her pale cheeks before popping open.

"Good girl."

Her crooked little smile was nearly enough to melt his heart.

Things were about to get a bit intense though, so concentrating on the task at hand was of the utmost importance. Craig didn't know Shelby as well as he'd like before playing, but there was no way in hell he was going to let the chance at touching her pass him by.

With steady fingers, he trailed her collarbone until it met shoulder, then continued to ply her silky flesh in circular motions before reaching the rope-entrapped tip of one breast.

Testing her pain tolerance, Craig pinched her rope-clamped nipples, watching for her reaction, loving her deep inhalation of breath as well as the small gasp to leave her plump lips.

"Like that?"

When she took too long to answer, he flicked the peak closest to him with the tip of his finger. Shelby's gaze flew to his, focusing. "Wh-what?"

"I asked you a question, little one. Do you like that?"

"Oh God! Yes...Sir."

"Would you like more?" Craig continued to stimulate her engorged nipples in soft, sensuous swirls with the tip of a single finger.

"Yes, Sir."

"Yes Sir, what?" Craig pushed. He could tell Shelby was uncomfortable with being vocal about her needs. She was obviously out of her element and yet trying so hard to please him. She was so damn hot he was afraid he might come without so much as a touch from her sweet, soft lips.

"I... Ahhhh."

She closed her eyes when he tugged gently where the rope passed across her nipples. It was his finger applying pressure over Shelby's clit that gained her attention.

When the beautiful green orbs of her eyes flashed open and she was once again focused intently on him, Craig spoke. "Tell me what you want, Shelby."

"I want more. I wa-want your touch. All over."

Craig smiled. Much better. He let up on the rope but kept his finger on her clit, merely lightening the pressure.

"Good girl."

The scent of her cream-slick cunt permeated the air around them, drawing Craig in, making him crazy with the need to swipe his tongue down the length of her puffy outer lips before rolling the swollen bud of her clit gently between his teeth. He wanted Shelby frantic with the need to come. Then and only then could he teach her a lesson in control.

Putting thought into action, Craig shifted position until his face was at the apex of Shelby's sprawled thighs. His hot breath caused her to squirm in vain in what he assumed was an attempt to get closer to his mouth.

"I'm going to lick every sweet inch of your juicy little pussy, baby. I want you writhing with need, with the need to come, with the need to please me. But you can't come until I give you permission."

Her groan was throaty, coming from deep within, her frustration nearly palpable. "If you disobey me, you will be punished. Do you understand?"

Shelby's breath was bursting from her lungs in shallow pants of air. "Yes, Sir."

Craig settled his mouth over her core, flicking his tongue as deep as he possibly could into her depths. Her taste burst across his tongue, staggering him.

She tasted sweet and hot, a mixture so erotic he felt an inexplicable need to go deeper, get closer, claim her for his own no matter the cost to either of them.

It was Shelby's whispered plea announcing the impending orgasm about to rack her body that finally pulled Craig from the depths of her cream-soaked cunt.

"Not yet, little one. Hold it back."

She thrashed as much as the ties binding her would allow. Craig could only guess at what her frenzied movements were causing the rope still imprisoning her nipples to do.

"I can't, I can't, I can't, I can't..." The chanted words as well as the bunching and tightening of her thigh muscles against his palms told Craig just how close she was to coming.

He continued to work her clit and the pretty pink folds now swollen with desire. Deepening his voice, Craig warned, "Don't you dare come without permission."

His words didn't seem to penetrate the fog of heat and need shrouding her, preparing her for the climax rapidly building in every cell of her body.

Craig slowed his torment of her clit. Once again lifting his mouth from her core, he spoke. "Look at me." His words insisted she listen, demanded it.

Her head rolled back and forth on the pillow. Each languid circle his finger made around her clit caused her to shiver anew.

"Now, Shelby!"

Something in the tone of his voice finally broke through whatever barrier surrounded her, causing Shelby to lift her head slightly, just enough for him to pin her with his gaze.

"You will do as I ask, Shelby, so concentrate."

She was going to kill him. Kill him and gut him and feed his balls to the wild animals. Of course, in order to do that he would have to stop and God only knew that was the last thing she wanted.

His finger passed across the ultra-sensitive swell of her clit, stealing her breath. The single torturous digit slowed for a brief second, just enough that she could catch her breath, before starting over. Around and around it went in ever-narrowing circles until once again moving right over her clit.

No longer could she think, understand or acknowledge what was happening to her. The only thing her body and mind would allow was for her to feel. Every nerve ending was alive.

Sensation so piercingly intense washed over her and for a minute Shelby thought she might faint from the overwhelming need for completion.

When the first peak of her orgasm got so close Shelby knew there was no holding it back, a strangled cry burst from her lips. Without thought to her actions, she shifted her hands from the headboard to the apex of her thighs, an unconscious plan to anchor them on Craig's head, to hold him where he was so she could ride the wave of her release with the warmth of his breath upon her.

Her impending climax ranked right up there with all things too good to be true. Before the first crest could cause her to tumble over, a sharp sting to her inner thigh pulled her from the warm crashing waves of what would surely have been the most intense release of her life.

To say she was pissed would be putting it mildly. It took a second for Shelby to gather her wits and realize the sting had come from an open-palmed swat delivered by Craig's hand, but when she did, the fight was on.

"What the fuck did you do that for?"

Not planned in the least and yet said all the same, the words tumbled from her mouth. Shelby's hair stuck to her face, uncomfortably irritating her more.

The expression on Craig's face warned Shelby she'd made a terrible mistake.

"Are you using your safe word?" Menacingly low, his voice promised punishment. And yet, there was no inner argument, no worries for her physical well being.

"No."

"You disobeyed by moving your hands. Your punishment was a swat to your thigh. The extent of your outburst will cost you even more."

Craig edged off the bed. It sounded as if he was rustling through his bag but from her bound vantage point, Shelby could not see what he was doing. The not knowing made her nervous, even a bit scared. Not enough to safe-word out or ask Craig what he was doing, but frightened nonetheless.

When he returned, his hands were full. Of what, Shelby had no idea. Without so much as a word, he eased back onto the bed, this time to sit between her widespread thighs.

She lifted her head from the mattress, wanting to know what he was doing. The view to greet her eyes caused a spiral of sensations to cascade one after another across her flesh.

His brown eyes bore into her as he tore open a box, removing a new purple butt plug, one that appeared to be ominously wide. He proceeded to spread lube across its tip.

Shelby wasn't sure whether she was tugging at her bonds in an attempt to gain her freedom or beg him to hurry the hell up. All she managed was a whimper of anguished need when he placed a single finger over the swollen bud of her clit.

"You belong to me right now, Shelby. Unless you safe-word out you will be experiencing a crash course in control. This..." Craig held up the lube-glistening plug for her inspection, "...will remind you with every movement of your body, with every thrust of my finger into your weeping pussy, to obey me."

They'd talked about her experiences, including anal play, but never in a million years had Shelby imagined Craig would venture there so early in the game.

When he lowered the plug between the cheeks of her ass, pressing it slowly into her, Shelby moaned. The feel of him touching her there was more intense, more private, more personal than she could have ever imagined. Anal play and sex were something she had always enjoyed, possibly even loved, but never before had it hit her with the intensity it did now.

A burning desire to please him overcame Shelby with a force unlike anything she'd ever before experienced while bottoming. It was getting very hard to remember she was not a submissive, merely someone who enjoyed kinky play.

Doing the best she could to accommodate the plug slowly invading her most private of places, Shelby gulped a deep breath.

"That's it, little one. Breathe and relax. You can do it, baby."

She would do it, dammit. She'd do it and love it. A streak of fire shot through her as Craig steadily pressed until the widest part of the plug stretched the tight ring of muscle protecting the delicate entrance of her ass.

A low moan, a combination of pain and pleasure, welled up from deep within, spilling across her dry lips. The press of his finger as it relentlessly circled her clit only added to the delicious torment.

It was about that time Shelby realized she was beyond screwed. Hoping a change in attitude would do the job or that Craig got off on hearing a woman's plea for release, Shelby begged.

"Oh God! Please...please may I come, Sir?"

Shelby's words seemed to have the complete opposite effect of what she had hoped for. No more than a heartbeat of time passed before Craig's answer made her want to scream.

"Not without permission." He followed the clipped response with an increase of not only pressure but speed with which he was torturing her clit.

"Concentrate, baby. Hold on for me, for my pleasure."

His words somehow lowered a veil of calm over her, sending Shelby on a floaty ride inside of her own body. The sensations cascading over every inch of her, coursing through her veins, were still intense, still relentless and yet she no longer had any doubt she could do it, would do it.

For her Master.

Time seemed to stop as did anything resembling a coherent thought. Something was wrong with what her mind had just worked out, but for the life of her, Shelby couldn't quite grasp what it was. There was no time to dwell on it when the intensity of Craig's voice insisted she listen and obey.

"Come for me, Shelby. Come now!"

Her old life burst into a million shattering pieces, releasing something new. Something from deep within her. Something that, due to the encroaching blackness, Shelby would have to wait to come to terms with.

Chapter Four

Shelby was fiery in her submission, fighting it halfway while trying with her other half to accept who and what she was.

To come to terms with and be okay with submission in a politically correct world where women were taught never to submit had to be a daunting task. He shook such thoughts from his mind. Now was not the time. Not when Shelby lay curled in his arms, no longer bound to the bed for his pleasure but instead receiving the best aftercare he could give.

Craig brushed her hair from her face. The flush of Shelby's cheeks was in complete contrast with the near stillness of her breathing.

"You have no idea how much you please me."

Merely snuggling closer to his chest, she said not a word. Her body was limp and pliant, restful in its repose. Craig could only imagine how exhausting it was to submit as thoroughly as she had.

Although he had no doubt she had tried to hold back as long as possible, he was fairly sure they'd connected on a much deeper level than anything Shelby had ever before experienced. Craig planned to make sure it happened over and over and over again. He knew now more than ever exactly how right she was for him.

Even when angry at her unwillingness to believe in herself and her newfound submissiveness, it was obvious that Shelby was more than the players who insisted they were slave material, needing ownership.

What Shelby was came naturally and from deep within. It was in every inch of her flesh, each drop of blood, whether she wanted to believe it or not.

Craig sighed in relief that things had gone so well. She'd submitted completely to him, her eyes telling a deep and emotional story, locking with his just as she'd climaxed.

It was more than Craig had hoped for. He would take everything she gave, pushing her limits and binding her with the touch of his hand. Shelby would grow to crave his touch as much as he already craved her. Hopefully love would follow.

"Come on, little one." Craig caressed her a bit more insistently, his plan to wake her in a gentle manner.

As much as he hated the thought, she needed more than just the thin blanket he'd wrapped her in at the end of their scene. She needed clothes, food and water and then they would talk.

Spreading kisses across her forehead before moving down to her mouth, Craig enjoyed the taste of her pale flesh. He wanted to take her home and devour her, to show her the private playroom his house boasted. The special place where he took few to play and so far none who mattered as Shelby already did.

When she didn't budge, Craig sat up, jostling her in his arms. The fun was over and aftercare begun. He would kick his own ass if anything negative were to happen to her after an experience with him. No passing out on his watch.

Craig stood Shelby in front of him. With his hands clasped around her waist, he made sure her legs were steady enough for her to hold her own weight. Her green eyes flashed open. She appeared a bit disoriented before a look of awareness crossed her features.

"You need a snack and something to drink, baby." Craig removed his hands from Shelby's waist, hating the loss of her heat against his palms.

With a hand at her elbow, he guided her out of the private room they had been occupying and into the main dungeon area of the club. When she stopped dead in her tracks, Craig turned to see what had caused the sudden change of pace.

She was staring at him while clutching the thin blanket around her arms in a way Craig could only describe as defensive. Her wide eyes were shuttered, closing him off from her thoughts, her feelings, just as she'd tried to do early on in their session.

No fucking way in hell was he going to let her get away with shutting him out. Just the thought of Shelby's attempt to do so made Craig's hand tingle with the need to spank her ass.

"Let's go." His words were clipped, curt to the extreme as he led her through the main room and into a side room where she could change in private.

Shelby eyed the front door as she took her clothes from him.

"Don't even think about it, little one."

Craig had to respect the fact that she didn't try to pretend to misunderstand what he was saying. Instead, the fiery minx edged her chin up at a defiant angle and looked him dead in the eye before pushing past him and into the room.

The door closing echoed through his mind. The snick of the lock against its mooring made him want to break through the physical barrier, take her in his arms and once again show Shelby who she really was.

Curling his hands into tight fists, Craig did his best to ignore the urge. To do so would only prove how out of control he felt and that was not an option for a man like himself, one who made a living out of being in complete control.

It was disturbing just how much a tiny little slip of a woman could damn near bring him to his knees. A few years back, Craig would have refused to play with her. The hold she had over him was too strong and way too unsettling, especially given she was clueless about her importance in his future.

His patience was running thin, with both himself and Shelby. "Either you come out or I'm coming in."

Mere seconds passed before the door swung open. Her rounded chin was still inched high, adding to the mutinous look on her dimpled cheeks. Had he not noticed the red rimming her eyes, Craig very well may have spanked her ass then and there.

For now, she was off the hook. She would get her punishment and take it as any wayward submissive should, of that there was no doubt. But right now was not the time.

"Let's grab you a drink and snack, little one."

Craig did his best to keep the anger and impatience out of his voice. Her luminescent eyes and the nearly unnoticeable quiver of her bottom lip warned him to keep things calm.

First off, he knew she was more than likely having a bit of trouble coping with all that had happened in such a short time. What really sent him staggering though was how much the sight of her teary eyes turned him on.

Once again Craig was hard as a rock. Just thinking about protecting Shelby, caring for her and bringing her to tears of frustrated pleasure as he bound her tightly with rope, sent blood rushing to his cock.

He snatched half a sandwich off a platter and a bottle of water out of an ice chest with Shelby in mind. He handed her both without a word.

She took them from his hand, trying her best not to touch him. When she had the food held within her grasp, Shelby turned to him. "I'm ready to go home now."

It took every ounce of willpower Craig had to escort her to the door without first finding an empty room where he could spank her ass until it was beet red before sliding his cock deep within its tight, forbidden depths. He wanted to brand her as his, lord his dominance over her. Insist she accept everything he offered then beg for more.

Instead he walked her to her car. When she was seated inside, he reached across to buckle her seat belt. Once done, Craig leaned in close.

"This is not over, Shelby. Not even close to being over. As a matter of fact, it's just beginning."

With a hand anchored in the curls of her hair, he angled her head sharply for his kiss, increasing the intensity with which he held her, causing her to gasp, opening her mouth.

Her taste only hammered home just how willing he was to pursue her until she understood her submissive nature. After that if she decided she wanted nothing to do with him, then so be it, but for now she owed it to herself to at least face the truth.

Before closing the door, Craig warned, "Don't make me come for you, little one."

Ω

Even after two days Shelby's body still ached deliciously. Every twinge reminded her of exactly what had happened, how Craig had played her body, controlling everything from her words and thoughts to her orgasms.

Coming out of the haze of lust and submission that had overcome her mind, body and soul two days ago had left her shaken and confused.

Shelby had played before. She'd experienced wonderfully intense orgasms at the hands of men who were sought after for their ability to wield a single tail whip. Being tied by some of the most talented in the art of Japanese rope bondage, also known as Shibari, rated extremely high on her list, especially given her love for rope.

And yet, not one of those experiences could have prepared her for being bound and at Craig's mercy. There was no way she could have prepared for the emotions that had run through her body. And there was definitely no way she could have prepared for the rollercoaster of feelings that the last two days had thrust upon her.

Craig had taken care of her, held her until her body stopped trembling.

He had been patient, waiting for what, Shelby still wasn't sure, but something in his gaze, as she left, warned just how serious he was. If she did not go to him, he would surely come for her.

And then what?

Shelby didn't want to find out that way. Confronting an angry Craig was not something she relished the idea of. No, she would call the club and speak with him in order to get his address and let him know she'd be by to see him first thing in the morning.

Too bad she hadn't come to the conclusion a bit sooner, before Craig's shiny black truck pulled up to the front door of the lakeside cottage she was using for the summer.

"Damn, damn, damn."

Shelby muttered the words beneath her breath as Craig made his way up the walkway. Not wanting to be inside alone with him, she opened the door before he had the chance to knock. Making her way out, she closed it securely behind her.

His movements were swift, soundless as he stepped onto the porch to stand directly in front of her. Taking her in his arms, Craig buried a hand deep within her hair and slanted his mouth over hers.

The kiss was mind numbing. Passion and power dueled with heat so intense Shelby felt it in every atom of her being. His tongue fought its way into her mouth, stroking against her, tasting and teasing until she thought she might die from the sheer pleasure.

Tingles of delight walked their way up and down her spine, radiating out to her nipples, peaking them with desire. The full length of his body was plastered against her, showing Shelby just how much she affected him.

The thought made her happy for some off-the-wall reason. She was leery about admitting her submissiveness, about the idea of belonging wholly to only one man, but the thought of pleasing Craig both sexually and in other aspects of his life gave her great joy.

He separated their mouths, breaking the kiss, all without releasing the hold he had on her hair. His brown eyes bore into her, asking questions Shelby wasn't sure she had answers to.

Although she'd already made up her mind to belong to Craig if that was truly what he wanted, Shelby still had a few things to work out in her head, to search her soul for.

If he wanted her, all of her, Craig would have to understand and allow her one more night.

"I wanted to come see you." Shelby did her best to keep her voice even. It was a hard thing to accomplish considering all the emotions roiling around inside of her. It would be so easy to second-guess her decision. Shelby worried what others might think when she agreed with everything in her to belong to a man widely known in the community for his activities in and with a club like Club Jerico.

She could very well use it as an excuse. The problem was the only thing she would accomplish by doing so would be to shortchange herself on what would surely be a life-altering experience.

Having met Craig, it was something Shelby was not willing to chance.

"Then why didn't you?" Before she could answer, he added, "I warned you not to make me come after you and yet, here I am."

An ominous tone laced his voice. Something in it told Shelby she would be paying in some way.

"I didn't want to go back to the club just yet. I wanted to go to your place. But I don't know where you live. Tomorrow morning I was going to find you." Her voice was starting to tremble just slightly. Shelby hated the telltale sign of her nervousness.

A perplexed look in Craig's gaze said he wasn't quite sure he believed her. His next question proved that beyond a shadow of a doubt. "And you didn't think to call?" There was a dangerous edge to his voice. It wasn't anger, more like skepticism, as if he thought she might be lying to him.

"I wasn't sure if I was ready."

Shelby wasn't sure she could say the words yet, to admit she was his, that she belonged to him. Then the uncertainty of the situation got the best of her and Shelby could no longer hold her tears at bay.

Could it be that he merely felt slighted by how quickly she'd left? Maybe he only wanted a play partner. God how she hated the not knowing and the emotional turmoil it brought with it.

Shelby felt as though she were fluttering in the breeze. Would Craig be her anchor or would a strong wind carry her away? She sniffled then gave a little hiccough. What a mess she was making of things.

Craig gathered her close to his body. The heat of him warmed her from the inside out. "So you don't know if you're ready to admit you're mine?"

He asked the question so sincerely, so quietly, Shelby had to struggle to hear the words. She shook her head against his chest, hiding her face from his possible reaction. In her mind Shelby already knew she was his. Admitting it openly was where she was having trouble. Craig seemed to understand.

"I won't push right now. It sounds as though you've got a bit more thinking to do." He kept her close, one hand in her hair, the other rubbing sensuous circles along her back.

After a moment, Craig held her at arm's length. This time when he spoke, his voice poured over her, spreading warmth through Shelby, body and soul.

"You might not be ready to admit the truth to me, and I'm okay with that for right now, but are you ready to learn I mean what I say? That when I give a warning it should be heeded?"

Hearing him speak of her punishment for making him come for her had Shelby so freaking hot she thought she might spontaneously combust.

"Yes, Sir."

She knew her eyes were wide as saucers, more than likely giving her a deer in the headlights look, but just thinking about the possibilities had her dripping wet and nervous as hell.

"Then invite me in, little one."

Chapter Five

Craig watched as Shelby reached for the doorknob, her fingers trembling. He hoped her nervousness came from a multitude of emotions, including a good amount of arousal.

Once through the door, Shelby stepped aside. The look on her face told him she was waiting, unsure of what his next move would be. He wanted to keep her waiting for a little bit longer.

Keeping her off kilter would only add to the intensity of the erotic spanking he planned to use as punishment. Of course, punishment was far from what was truly about to happen.

Craig eyed her drawstring pants and T-shirt with contempt. He wanted her out of them, now, ready for his touch, his pleasure.

"Stand over there." He motioned to the center of the room.

With her hands clasped in front of her, she moved in the direction he'd instructed. Once there, she stopped and slowly turned to face him.

"Take your shirt off, little one."

Craig kept his voice low, commanding. It was hard considering what he really wanted to do was stalk his way across the room, rip her clothes from her body and plunge the length of his rock-hard cock deep into the tight confines of her pretty pink pussy.

Doing so would only mess things up and he knew it. Shelby craved the control he promised, insisted upon. She would thrive as his slave, loved and cherished beyond all else. Soon. Very soon, Craig reminded himself.

She inched her shirt up, showing first her midriff then her breasts, which were gloriously unencumbered. They bobbed free of the cotton T-shirt as if glad to be uncovered.

"Now your pants."

Once again, she did as asked. He could only find fault in the fact that Shelby did not give him the benefit of an answer, including the title he so loved to hear slip from her lips.

She was so damned giving, so beautiful in her submissiveness that Craig wanted to gather her up in his arms and whisk her away to his personal playroom where he could do all sorts of kinky things with her gorgeously curvy body.

When the full globes of her ass peeked above the waistband of her pants, Craig had trouble holding back a groan of frustration. As she reached for the waistband of her g-string panties, Craig stopped her.

"Leave those on."

She gave him a strange look for the briefest of seconds before dropping her hands.

"You are so hot, baby. You have no idea how much I want to fuck you right now." It was an admission, one that added a bit of spunk to her movements.

Craig couldn't help but chuckle. "Of course, that isn't going to happen just yet." He shook his head sadly. "Nope, first we've got a lesson to learn."

Looking around, Craig found exactly what he was searching for, a low-backed kitchen chair. After pulling several fairly short lengths of rope from his coat pocket, he removed the coat.

He laid it neatly across the back of one chair, his movements achingly slow in hopes of adding to the arousal, the amount of emotion whirling around inside of Shelby.

Once done, he moved back to where Shelby still stood motionless, watching, chair in hand. "Bend over the back of this, little one."

Her green-eyed gaze swung to the chair, then back to him, but her feet stayed rooted in place. Instead of helping her with a stinging swat to the ass, something she was setting herself up for extra of anyway, he decided a bit of coaxing might work better.

"Come on, Shelby. The sooner we get this part over with, the sooner we can move on to the good stuff."

His words must have spoken volumes because without wasting any more time, she did as he asked. Arching herself over the back of the chair, she braced her hands against the armrests.

With methodical motions, Craig slowly and carefully secured each wrist with a length of rope. He checked the tightness, then sensually slid his fingers along Shelby's arm.

Craig knelt behind her, making sure the warmth of his breath could be felt along her thighs as he tied her ankles to opposite chair legs. The position she was in left her open and vulnerable to his every whim.

"Comfortable?" He asked the question already knowing the answer so was not at all surprised by her answer.

"No."

Craig swatted her ass. "No what?"

"No, S-Sir."

The feel of her ass beneath his palm was so damned erotic he wasn't at all sure he was going to last very long. Denying himself the pleasure of touching her more intimately, of kneeling behind her to taste of her sweetness, Craig instead continued peppering her ass.

The first swats were designed to warm up flesh unused to such treatment. Those that followed were intended to sting, to burn, to remind.

"Oh! P-please. Please touch me."

Craig landed a blow just a bit harder than the rest, then rubbed the offended flesh, which was now red hot.

"But I am touching you, little one."

Her whimper of frustration was like music to his ears.

"I need more. Please, please, please."

Shelby's words made his pulse race. Perspiration dotted his forehead and for a moment Craig thought about calling a halt to it all. He wanted to take her and make her his, to brand her body with his come, to mark her with more than just his handprints.

Shelby worried she might have gone too far in asking for more. Hell, she couldn't even remember to call him Sir, what in the world made her think she deserved anything other than what he was already offering?

Her bound wrists chafed, shoulders ached and her ass was on fire and yet, she felt free and relaxed. It was simply amazing.

She was just starting to feel a bit smug about the whole idea of punishment and what she could handle when Craig moved in behind her. The heat of his jean-clad pelvis against her ass was like adding flame to an already-burning fire.

The whimper of pain and pleasure that escaped her closed lips was so animalistic it took Shelby a minute to realize it came from her.

When Craig reached around her upper body to play with her nipples, squeezing them tight between his thumb and forefinger, her head began to swim.

"Oh. Oh yes. *Yessss!*" The words were released on a hissed breath. Her core ached to be filled, touched, licked. Anything.

Oh God but she wanted him to finish her. The only problem was she would not ask nor beg. She was bound and determined to play by Craig's rules. It was the only way she could think of to prove just how much she wanted to serve him, needed to be with him.

Had she not been bound to the chair, Shelby very well may have fallen to the floor in a boneless twitching heap when he finally snaked a hand down her back, fingering the crack of her ass as he continued to move down to her sex.

It seemed as if he were moving in slow motion. His talented fingers plunged into her pussy only to back out dripping with her juice before stroking her clit to attention. Several times she got so close to coming she was sure nothing would stop the ensuing climax, only to be pulled short by a sharp swat to her inner thigh.

"Don't you dare come without my permission, Shelby. This is not about your pleasure. It's about your punishment. You'll take what I give you and not a bit more. Do you understand?"

Part of her wanted to call him every name in the book. That was the smart-assed part she'd always used to hold at bay those who were getting too close. It was the other part she was going to listen to today though, the one that wanted nothing more than to please the man behind her. To see a wide smile on his lips and hear his words of praise when all was said and done.

Coming to a quick decision on the matter, Shelby answered, "Yes, Sir. I understand."

"Good, baby. Real good."

His words of praise caused a smile to curve her lips, but only briefly. When Craig began untying her, Shelby felt an unexplainable urge to cry. She blinked rapidly, fighting the need with all her might.

Once she was free, Craig helped her to stand. She was so hot and horny it took everything in her not to pounce on him. Her body, unused to the position she'd been bound in, protested every movement.

Shelby wasn't sure if it was her groan of discomfort or the grimace plastered across her face that caught Craig's attention but without a word, he began massaging her shoulders and arms with vigorous sweeps of his hands.

"Better, little one?" He stared at her as if he could see straight into her heart and decipher the secrets of her soul.

"Much better. Thank you, Sir."

His smile was magnificent, the pleasure in his eyes a sight to behold. Tomorrow she would belong to this man mind, body and soul. Tonight was wonderful, even if done in the need for discipline, but tomorrow, tomorrow Shelby would start anew, a rebirth of sorts. A time when she would no longer deny her nature or withhold her love or emotions.

A very scary thought to say the least, one she wouldn't dwell on any more tonight.

Craig's hand in her hair brought Shelby's mind back to what was happening. "Are you wet for me, baby?"

Shelby nodded the best she could with her head anchored so tightly in his grasp. Was he finally going to fuck her? *Oh please let that be the case,* she thought, afraid to voice the words.

"Show me."

His orders confused her. She wasn't at all sure how he meant. "How?"

"Touch yourself and show me, little one. I want to see your fingers glisten with your cream. I want proof of just how much you want my touch."

The wicked words rolled around in her head. This one was easy. Touching herself was something Shelby had no trouble with. She knew exactly what she liked, so masturbating was something she did often.

She looked Craig in the eye as she slid a hand down her abdomen to the apex of her thighs, where she dipped two fingers into the heat of her body. She was so wet she could smell her scent in the air. It surrounded them as did the slick sounds of her fingers moving over her flesh.

Unable to help the heat invading her cheeks, Shelby felt the blush that was more than likely as red as her ass cross her face. She lifted her finger coated in the proof of her desire as an offering to Craig.

"Good girl. Now taste yourself."

This time his instructions made her decidedly uncomfortable. When she balked, Craig arched an eyebrow but remained silent. It took Shelby a minute to work up the nerve to take on such an intimate task but figured at this point in the game, refusing would likely just end with her back over the chair.

"Mmmmm. You are so damned hot."

Using his hand in her hair to guide, Craig motioned Shelby to her knees. His pants were open, the thick length of his cock free.

"I want you to play with your pussy while you suck me, little one. Keep it wet and hot, baby, but no coming."

Excited beyond belief, Shelby did as asked. The minute her mouth closed around the head of Craig's cock, exquisite taste burst on her tongue. His scent filled her nostrils as she struggled to take him deeper while playing with the slick folds of her pussy.

She was unsure if it was her excitement and the need to come or wanting so desperately to please Craig, but the sounds emanating from him told her she was doing a great job.

"Fuck yeah."

His hold on her hair tightened, pulling as his hips bucked, sinking his length so deep she gagged. Tears rolled down her cheeks but there was nothing she could do about them, nothing she wanted to do, at least not until he came.

"Just like that, Shelby. Suck me deep. Take me. Take all of me."

The last was said on a grunt, a sound of sheer pleasure as his cock swelled in her mouth before filling it with his essence.

Shelby continued to play with herself as she swallowed every last drop Craig's body offered. She was so hot and so freaking ready to come she thought she might faint from the agony of holding back.

Craig, on the other hand, seemed completely content. He backed away, pulling his now flaccid shaft from her lips, then proceeded to fasten his pants.

"Stop."

It seemed as if he were speaking a foreign language. "Wh-what?"

"I said stop." He lowered his gaze to where her fingers still busily stroked the folds of her greedy sex. "Don't make me ask you a second time, little one."

He had to be kidding.

Oh please let him be kidding!

When Craig helped Shelby to her feet, she knew it wasn't to be. Holding back tears of frustration was a very hard thing to do. So was not coldcocking him then kicking his cruel ass out of her house.

"You have things to think about, if I remember right, so I'll be leaving now. I never want it to be said that I influenced your decisions one way or the other." He took the time to write his home address on a piece of paper. His calmness irritated Shelby beyond belief.

"You're going to just leave me like this?" Shelby was extremely frustrated. Her body ached for more, wept with need, a need it seemed was not going to be met.

"I am. And the next time you think to disobey me, you'll remember today."

Craig stepped forward and gathered Shelby in his arms, kissing her slow and deep. After pulling his mouth from hers, he raised her hand to his lips and, one by one, suckled the fingers she'd used to pleasure herself.

"Remember, you don't come without my permission. I'll know if you do." With those words he turned and headed to the door, calling over his shoulder as he stepped across the threshold, "See you tomorrow, little one."

Chapter Six

The sight of her flushed cheeks wouldn't leave Craig's mind. He hadn't slept a wink, hating having left Shelby in such a state of arousal. In his need to teach the little minx a bit of control, Craig was losing most of his.

Life was known for throwing curves, but this time around, it seemed like he was getting nothing but hairpin turns.

Would she show up? He thought so, was almost sure. Of course, leaving the way he had last night had very obviously pissed Shelby off. The mutinous expression to cross her pixie-like features nearly made him chuckle. It was clear she'd wanted to do some physical harm to his person.

The humor quickly died when Craig realized it was already going on noon and Shelby had yet to make an appearance. What would he do if she didn't show?

Nothing.

The thought almost buckled his knees but there was little he could do about it. If she didn't show it was for a reason. Perhaps she wasn't quite ready for the level of relationship he expected and if that was the case, things between them would go downhill very fast.

It was a slippery slope Craig didn't even want to consider.

If she decided not to show he was left no alternative but to let her go. His mind screamed at the injustice of the offending thought, but trust was the key to any relationship, especially a BDSM relationship. If he pursued when she clearly didn't want what he offered, then he would jeopardize the trust they had already established.

One thing he wasn't willing to overlook were the rules of Safe, Sane and Consensual. Take away one and the cycle would be broken. It was something Craig wouldn't do. It would go against everything in him. No, he would just wait and pace like the caged animal he felt inside.

Nearly another hour passed before he heard it, a very light, very tentative knock at his front door. Shelby.

He stalked across the living room to the front door, a bit angry because he'd been made to wait. The thought of possibly being played crossed his mind, making Craig realize how much he cared. More than likely too much and too soon.

The minute Craig saw Shelby's face, her pale cheeks and teary green eyes, his anger drained away.

"Come here, little one."

There was nothing more important than holding her, letting her know just how safe she was with him, even when he wanted to claim her in every way a man could possibly claim a woman.

She clung to him, burrowing her face into his chest as if trying to climb inside. "You're safe here, Shelby. You know that, right?" With a finger beneath her chin, Craig tipped her face up for his perusal.

"Yes, Sir. I do." Shelby spoke quietly, solemnly, but with an underlying strength that made Craig proud.

"Good girl."

This time a bright smile curved her pillow-soft lips. When she backed out of his grasp, Craig had to fight the urge to anchor her to him, to hold her tight and never allow her out of his reach. That, of course, was impossible and he knew it so made no move to stop her when she backed away from him.

Shelby's next actions moved Craig, awed him in a way so unexpected he felt lightheaded. Without a word of instruction from him, she lifted the knee-length dress she was wearing over her head, leaving her completely bare, gloriously naked to his gaze.

When she knelt before him, her ass in the air, cheek to the floor and arms stretched high above her head, Craig nearly swallowed his tongue. The position was extremely submissive. Done voluntarily as she had, without his coaxing or insistence, made it such a wonderful gift.

Craig did the first thing that came to mind. He dropped to his knees beside Shelby. Stroking the length of her back, he ended at the base of her skull where he buried a hand in her hair.

"Thank you, little one."

Lifting her head, he stared deeply into her eyes. The kiss to follow was awkward due to the strange position Shelby was in, but it mattered very little. The taste of her submission on his tongue was like heaven and hell all rolled into one.

"Get up, baby."

Craig helped Shelby to her feet. She had a dazed look about her. Not like she was having second thoughts, more like she couldn't believe she had actually worked up the nerve to do what she was doing.

"You okay?"

He asked the question out of genuine concern. Her whispered, *"Yes, Sir"* went straight to his cock, causing it to swell and lengthen even further.

Craig laced his fingers with hers, then pulled her up the hall after him. There were a couple of things he had to be sure of, a few things he wanted to do before he took her to his bed—a place no other woman had been invited—and make her his for all time.

When they reached the door to his private playroom, Craig removed a key from his pocket. After unlocking the door, he pushed it wide. Shelby's eyes appeared huge in her round face. This time Craig couldn't help but chuckle.

Her reaction pleased him greatly. If there was one thing Craig enjoyed it was this room, a room he'd designed and lovingly built with every possible means of erotically torturing the woman who would be his.

"Go on in and have a seat." He motioned for her to sit on the rather large table dominating the center of the room. "I'll be right back."

Craig didn't wait around to see if Shelby did as told, he just assumed she would. It was a test of sorts, albeit a simple one.

The sound of his shoes padding up the carpeted hallway echoed throughout the room like a gunshot. Where was he going and what was he going to do when he got there?

Trying her best to ignore the million and one thoughts whirling around in her head, she moved across the room to the table where she was expected to sit.

The surface was smooth metal that gleamed even in the dim light of the room. There were straps on all four corners and wide leather belts placed strategically along the sides. It resembled a physician's table with no stirrups. For that, Shelby was grateful.

When Craig made his way back to her he was wearing nothing more than a robe and holding a bottle of water.

"Tell me why you're here."

His question was blunt and to the point but Shelby was prepared, ready to answer.

"Because I trust you with my life. I want to belong to you. In my mind, I am already yours…" She took a deep, fortifying breath, then finished, "…Master."

His reaction was swift. Instead of pouncing on her, strapping her to the table and having his way as she half expected, he moved in quick strides across the room to the armoire she hadn't yet noticed.

The room was a bit dark so Shelby could not see everything in it, but her mind had no trouble imagining the things hiding in there. When he came back to her it was with what could only be considered a cane in hand.

"And if I wanted to use this on you now?"

Shelby couldn't help the nervousness coursing through her system. She swallowed deeply and tried to remember to breathe. She had often read that any tool of the trade, even the mildest, could turn vicious in the wrong hands. That meant the same had to be true on the flip side, even the most vicious of tools, such as a cane, could bring pleasure when in the right hands.

"I would trust your judgment and do my best to please you."

Before she'd even completed her sentence, Craig dropped the cane. Gathering her in his arms, he stormed from the room. Shelby wondered where he was headed but with her face snuggled into his neck, his manly scent filling her lungs, she figured it didn't much matter.

When he carried her into his room and set her gently on the chocolate brown comforter covering the oversized four-poster, she was shocked.

Not only had she heard whispers of his wickedly stocked playroom but Shelby had also heard through the grapevine at Club Jerico how Craig never took a woman to his bed. Many had vied for the position but none had ever made it. And yet, here she sat.

"Look at me, little one."

Shelby didn't need any more prompting. Swinging her gaze his way, she waited, listened.

"This is new to me too." The admission seemed a bit hard for him but he continued. "I knew you were mine the minute I saw you on the floor wrapped in plastic. I'll never voluntarily release you so you have to be sure."

"I am sure, Master. More sure than I have ever been about anything in my life."

Craig climbed onto the bed beside her, several lengths of black rope clutched in his hand. He stroked the lengths almost lovingly with his free hand while watching her intently.

Leaning forward, he bestowed her with a kiss so deep and soul shattering Shelby wasn't sure she'd ever recover. The words he whispered in her ear were so much more than a declaration of love. They were an understanding, a new beginning. The completion of a circle.

The ropes fell to the wayside as he gathered her hands in his. With their fingers entwined, he pinned Shelby's arms beside her head. The feel of his body full on hers, nude and hot, was glorious.

"Open for me, little one."

His voice was a rough whisper. He released her hands just long enough to sheathe the burgeoning length of his cock, protecting them, before once again pinning her arms to the mattress.

Shelby needed to feel him in her, craved his dominance more than she needed her next breath. She did as he asked, spreading her thighs wide. When she felt the head of his cock at her entrance, she couldn't help but arch her back, offering all she was to the man who had somehow managed to steal her heart.

Craig's face was a mask in concentration. Sweat dotted his forehead and his arms shook.

"I'm sorry, baby. I wanted to make this nice for you."

The words had no more left his lips then he plunged his entire length into her, stealing her breath, tearing a scream of unadulterated need from her lungs.

"If I wanted nice I would have stayed vanilla."

Their movements became frenzied, their scent filled the room and added to the sensations coursing through every cell of her body.

"Can I come? Please. Pleasepleaseplease."

Shelby's chanted words echoed off the walls. For a minute she wasn't sure she would be able to hold off. Craig's words of praise came just in time. "Good girl. Come for me now."

Needing nothing more than to hear Craig's voice speak the words giving her permission, Shelby's inner muscles tightened around his cock, milking its length. The sound of his voiced shout of completion echoing through the room was like music to her ears.

She didn't have time to come down from the first orgasm before the feel of Craig's length swelling inside her set off another. Once again, wave after wave of pleasure racked Shelby's body, claiming her senses until it felt as if there was nothing left in the world but the two of them.

Later that night, as they lay entwined together, rope completely forgotten, Craig spoke, his voice raspy with sleep.

"The answer to the question is…mine. Always mine, little one."

Shelby laughed in sheer delight. No longer would she wonder, *Your rope or mine?*

About the Author

Maggie Casper's life could be called many things but boring isn't one of them. If asked, Maggie would tell you that blessed would more aptly describe her everyday existence.

Being loved by four gorgeous daughters should be enough to make anybody feel blessed. Add to that a bit of challenge, a lot of fun and an undeniably close circle of friends and family and you'd be walking in her shoes.

A love of reading was passed on by Maggie's mother at a very early age, and so began her addiction to romance novels. Maggie admits to writing some in high school but when life got in the way, she put her pen and paper up. Seems that things changed over the years because when she finally decided it was time to put her story ideas on paper, the pen was out and the computer was in. Took her a while to catch up but she finally made it.

When not writing, Maggie can usually be found reading, doing genealogy research or watching NASCAR.

To learn more about Maggie, please visit www.maggiecasper.com. Send an email to Maggie Casper at maggie@maggiecasper.com or join her Yahoo! group to join in the fun with other readers as well as Maggie Casper http://groups.yahoo.com/group/sultrysiren.

Look for these titles by
Maggie Casper

Now Available:

California Cowboy
Chance of a Lifetime
Every Beat of Her Heart
For the Love of Callie
Something Old, Something New
Teaching Elena

Ladies! Meet Red Hot Alaskan Men

Nancy Lindquist

Dedication

To Bunti. Living life in the last frontier, and loving it! I'm so glad we bonded in the parking lot nightmare. Also to Cruise Critic. Thanks for supplying me with my dearest friends. Bet you never thought you'd be mentioned in an erotic romance!

Chapter One

The room buzzed with conversation, anticipation and promise. Chastity Cuthbert glanced around with a smile and pushed up the damn glasses that slid down her face for the umpteenth time tonight. Over one hundred well-dressed women milled around the refreshment table, held seats or chatted animatedly amongst themselves.

She peeked at her watch. Seven on the dot, perfect. She reached up to smooth the tightly coiled bun holding her hair in place at her nape, rubbed a finger over her teeth and stood with a smile. Heels clicking, she made her way to the microphone. *Ouch!* The stylish shoes pinched unbearably. She'd planned to wear something with a lower heel. Served her right for stopping by her neighbor, Freddie's apartment on her way out of the building.

She looked down and plucked a stray bit of fuzz from her sleeve. The damn glasses slid forward once more. Frowning, she shoved them back into place. *Of all the days to lose a contact.*

She tapped the mic. "Ladies, ladies. Can I have your attention please? If you'll all have a seat, we can begin."

She stood back, folded her arms, then remembered her last videotaped evaluation. With a sigh, she dropped them to her side. "Schoolmarmish." Eight of the ten evaluators had made it clear that she needed to get a handle on her personal style.

She'd received high marks for speech, word use and overall presentation, but her appearance... She smoothed the serviceable blue suit and mentally kicked herself. She should have listened to Freddie's advice about the red one she'd coveted at Carson's. At least the torturous shoes looked amazing.

The room around her settled into anxious giggles as nervous smiling women took their seats. She tried for an air of calm sympathy, and with a deep breath, glanced at her notes and began.

"I'd like to welcome everyone to this informational meeting for The Alaskan Connection. If you're not here to find the man of your dreams then allow me to direct you down the hall to Knitting 101." She waited for the expected titter to die down. "I'm Chastity and I'd like to show you why you're here." She pushed a switch on the podium, dimming the lights, and hit a key on her laptop. The screen behind her lit up with a ruggedly hunky smiling face. Oohs and ahs pelted her from all sides. She smiled. This was the best part of these meetings. Introducing the ladies to the natural wonders of the forty-ninth state.

She waited for the buzz to die down before continuing. "The Alaskan Connection prides itself on being the top matchmaking agency in Alaska. Each year we go to a different town, gather information on available men and bring that information back to you. Unlike other agencies, we run background checks on all perspective candidates. We want real romance for our clients and that's why, I'm happy to say, we have matched a record fifty-four percent of our clients within the first six months. The figures only get better after that." She clicked to another slide, this one of the gorgeous Alaskan wilderness.

"Does this sound like something you ladies are looking for?" Feminine cheers rose around her. She raised her hand for silence and continued the slideshow.

"Alaska is not for everyone. Harsh winters can make conditions brutal, but the rewards speak for themselves." Photos of her clients' weddings, with stunning scenery as a backdrop, beamed from the screen. Awestruck faces bloomed like flowers around her. Good, she'd sign up enough women tonight to make the trip a go and not have to put on any more presentations this season. She breathed a sigh of relief. She hated these sales talks. The butterflies never went away, no matter how many times she stood at a podium. Chastity much preferred the one-on-one matchmaking time and soothing her clients jangled nerves.

"I'm proud to say that this year our destination is..." she clicked once again, "...Smithfield, Alaska, population one thousand three hundred and six, and ladies, here's the best part. While the overall ratio of men to women in Alaska is eight men to every one woman, Smithfield's ratio is ten men to every woman. That's right. I said ten. Now I'd like to give you an opportunity to hear from a couple of my past clients. Rich and Lisa Murphy. Come on up, you two, and talk to these ladies."

She sat down, sipped her warm bottled water and waited while Rich and Lisa shared their love story. Normally she listened with rapt attention every time they told of their meeting, falling in love and subsequent marriage—she loved the romance, the joy on their faces, all of it. Tonight something felt off.

She glanced around. An uncomfortable feeling crawled over her skin, prickling it to goose bumps. Not the normal angst she felt speaking to a crowd, but something more. A woman shifted behind her and she caught a glimpse of a lone man in the crowd. She frowned. Men did not come to these seminars unless they were worried papas—this guy looked far too young to be the father of an adult woman. Something in his expression unnerved her and it wasn't his piercing gaze, alone.

The woman shifted back and Chastity lost sight of the man. She shrugged and turned back to face the stage. Silly—there was no other word for her feeling of foreboding. She must have imagined the irritation she thought she'd seen in his eyes.

The Murphys kissed. The applause of the crowd around her brought her to her feet. She mounted the stairs to the stage to hug Rich and Lisa. She turned back to the mic as they stepped off the stage and walked arm in arm to the back of the room. She smiled. They loved getting "outside" and visiting the lower forty-eight and she loved seeing them when they visited. *So in love.* Longing filled her heart, making it tough to draw a deep breath.

"Aren't they delightful? I'm thrilled to have had any part in bringing them together. Now I'm going to end this lecture and turn you loose. If you'd like to schedule a one-on-one meeting with me to discuss your interest in our summer trip, my four representatives are waiting at the long table in the back of the room. Each of these ladies has extensive training in psychology and matchmaking and can answer any of your questions, including those about fees. I will say that if you'd like to go with us this summer, you need to sign up soon. Only one hundred spaces are available for our next weeklong trip." She moved the slider on the dimmer, bringing the room lights up, and gestured to her employees who sat at long tables along one wall, waiting for the women who would soon swarm over them.

"I'd like to thank you for your time this evening and happy hunting." She clicked off the microphone. Whew. Another nerve-wracking presentation over. Maybe next year she'd hire someone to do these for her. She snorted. Who was she kidding? She was far too much of a control freak to ever let this portion of the business out of her hands. She gathered her notes in a neat pile and glanced around the podium for any scraps of paper she might have left behind.

"Miss Cuthbert?" The unexpected voice, low, masculine and very sexy, washed over her like warm sunshine after a long winter. She glanced up. Her gaze slammed into the greenest pair of eyes she'd ever seen. Forest green. No, leaf green. No, that wasn't quite right either. Sea green? They seemed to be all the shades of cool restfulness rolled into one. Her gaze traveled lower to the soft, full mouth. It sat above a stubble-covered chin that looked carved of stone, and his shoulders... She mentally shook herself. If she didn't stop her cerebral exploration of this man she'd be gawking at the front of his pants before long.

"Miss Cuthbert?"

"Hmmm." She glanced up and up. *Heavens, he's tall.* With a swallow, she composed herself. "I'm Miss Cuthbert. Call me Chastity." She stuck out her hand.

He reached out to shake it, his long fingers and large hand swallowing her smaller one. Tingles raced up her arm. She dropped her gaze to their hands, fitting together perfectly, then looked back up into his eyes. For a moment she read confusion there, then amusement.

"Chastity?"

She blushed. "My parents watched a lot of Sonny and Cher when they were dating. And you are?"

"Dave Wellington."

She knit her brow. She knew that name, but from where?

Her confusion must have telegraphed itself. "I'm the mayor of Smithfield, Alaska."

Pulling her hand from his, she slapped her forehead. "Oh right. You were out of town when I did my initial assessments. Good to meet you, Dave. You flew a long way for an introduction. I'll be up in your neck of the woods in a few weeks." She smiled broadly.

His green-eyed gaze didn't quite meet hers. "Actually, that's what I need to talk to you about. Your visit. I tried to call, but you've been out."

She shrugged. "Sorry, that's the nature of this business. I spend eighty percent of the time traveling. I'm always drumming up clients or towns to visit. I don't get to spend a lot of time at home."

"May we talk in private? Can we go somewhere? For coffee maybe?"

She shook her head. "I need to be here to answer questions. Would you like to meet some of the ladies we're signing up?"

He frowned. The movement turned his face dark, dangerous and sensual. Chastity shivered. "I don't think you understand. This isn't a courtesy visit. I'm here to stop you from bringing these women to my town." He leaned in as he spoke, until he was uncomfortably close to Chastity.

She blinked up at him. "Pardon me?"

"I really would rather not do this here."

Numbly she nodded towards a door behind her. He gently steered her towards the kitchen.

"Oh, Chastity? Well...hello, aren't you a hunk. Is he yours?"

Chastity swallowed a groan. *Not now.* Poppy Sinclair, her most hopeful and hopeless client. She'd been a member of The Alaskan Connection for three years now. Never missed a trip or a new town and then chased every available man with the glee of a starving vampire in a blood bank. Chas winced as subtly as she could manage.

"I just want to say that I'm super excited about the trip this year. I think it's going to be a super good time and I just L.O.V.E. the thought of so many tasty men for us ladies to munch on. I'm sure this will just be a super summer for me. Don't you think so?"

Chastity pasted a professional smile on her lips. "I'm sure it will be, Poppy." Dave's hand bit into her elbow and she frowned back at him. *Bully.* Was he reminding her he was here? Like she could forget this he-hunk man who hung from her arm. "Um, Poppy, why don't you go over to Sue's table and talk to her about what your hopes are. I'm sure she'll have some good ideas to help you make this summer your last one with us."

The other woman made a face that would probably wrinkle her brow, if she wasn't careful about her four times yearly Botox injections. "My last? Are you kidding? And give up this all-you-can-eat buffet? No way, Chastity. I'm going to stay single forever. It's just super, all the attention I get up there in the wilds of Alaska."

Chas concentrated on the ole smile and nod. She was not in the mood to try to educate this woman about The Alaskan Connection's purpose. To get couples together for a long-term relationship or marriage. Not find them summertime playmates.

"Well...if that's your goal."

The other woman laughed. High and sharp, the sound grated on Chastity's already frazzled nerves.

"It sure is. Oh wait, I see Kelly Maloney." She waved a red-tipped hand in the air that jingled from what had to be five pounds of bracelets. Great, Kelly. That woman was all Chas needed to complete the night. Kelly complained bitterly that she'd never met a man worth seeing again and used the company's guarantee to keep coming back summer after summer. "Yoo-hoo, Kelly! Here I am." Poppy leaned in. "I better go and give Kelly a big hug or she'll never forgive me." She smiled up at Dave, batted her eyes and brushed a hand over his shoulder. "You, I'll find later. It's just a super night! Toodles."

Chas let out a breath and allowed the tall man to resume directing her into the kitchen. The swinging door waved closed behind them, leaving them in relative privacy. He turned her to face him and took a step back. Great, he was staring down onto the top of her head and all she could do was lean back and look up so high her neck would be kinked in the morning. Not exactly conducive to good conversation. Irritation climbed within her and she swallowed hard to push it back down and play nice.

"Well, what do you have to say for yourself?"

She narrowed her gaze in confusion. His folded arms pushed his biceps out in the most appealing way. *Shut up, Chas. This guy is not here looking for a date and especially not at you for a date.* "What do you mean, what do *I* have to say for *myself?* You're the one who dragged me into the kitchen. I'm listening." She crossed her arms and glared up his impossible length. She could be intimidating too.

The review comments about her appearance once again swam in her head and she hung her hands at her sides. *Shoot.* Oh well. Right now, she had a feeling schoolmarmish would be helpful. She re-crossed them.

He threw up his arms in obvious annoyance. "I was going to speak to your better nature, but after that little slide show, I'm not sure you have one. So I'll get right to the point."

"What the hell are you talking about?"

"I'm talking about asking you to pick some other town to inundate with your wild women from the lower forty-eight. *We* don't want you in Smithfield."

Was this guy for real? She dropped her head, reached up and rubbed at what felt like the beginning of the mother of all headaches. "I hate to argue with such underwhelming logic, but I was there last fall. We had two hundred men sign up for my program. That doesn't sound like the welcome mat was exactly pulled out from under me."

"That was then. The town council is no longer interested in your business. We've voted to keep you out."

Her blood began to simmer, but she clamped a lid on it. "Your council welcomed me with open arms last fall. They were one hundred percent behind this trip. They even assisted me with room reservations, all paid in advance by the way, and backed up with an ironclad signed contract. What happened?"

"What happened is that I came back from a fishing trip to find out my fellow townspeople had lost their damned minds. I talked some sense into them. There's no such thing as love at first sight, Miss Cuthbert. I'm not sure love even exists at all. You're selling snake oil to these women and the good men of *my* town and I won't stand for it."

"Did you use a stick on them when you talked sense into them? Because what you're doing here feels more like bullying and coercion, than a gentle lecture. Am I wrong?" She stepped forward, only to have his gaze bore into hers. The menace behind the glare felt real—a bit too real. She stepped back, one step, then two, running into the stainless-steel prep table. She reached behind to steady herself. The closed shutters separating the kitchen from the hall looked pretty flimsy. If she screamed... She glanced back into his eyes. On second thought, he appeared pissed, not menacing. Maybe if she heard him out without getting her back up, he'd say his piece and go away.

Damn he smelled good. A mixture of pine and something wild and sexy. Where the hell did that thought come from? She was losing it. The man was treating her like a four-year-old and she was busy analyzing his cologne? Yep, she was certifiable.

He ran a hand through his hair. The thick, shiny, brown mass curled at the ends, like he needed a haircut. She swallowed and tried to remember that this hunk was not playing nice.

"I'm sorry. I'm not trying to bully you. I just think this is a very bad idea." He actually looked contrite. Maybe she'd misjudged him?

"Why?"

"Why?"

"Yes, why do you think this is a bad idea?"

"We just put in a new dock for cruise ships this year. My saloon puts on a historical reenactment for the tourists. This summer will make or break our town. We can't have any distractions. The cruisers will be a tough crowd. We can't afford to lose those contracts."

She snorted. "I hardly think that a few women dating some of your men will wreck your business, or harm your town."

"Look, I didn't want to be blunt, but here it is. I don't need a bunch of empty-headed bimbos coming into my town and breaking the hearts of my men, just as we're switching from a mining-based economy to a tourist-based one. The trip is off. Find another town to storm with your red-lipped floozies."

She straightened in disbelief. "You have got to be kidding? What kind of talk is that? Are you even from this century? That sounds like something my grandpa would have said."

"I'm just trying to be nice and not call those women out there"—he stuck a thumb out in the general direction of the hall—"any more names."

She fluttered her hands in the air. "You didn't hold your tongue before." She moved forward and punctuated her words with finger pokes at his chest, her fear gone. "Look, *Mr.* Wellington. I've got contracts, they're signed and they're actionable, should you talk anyone into trying to duck out of them. I have interested men and I have women who are paying good money for an opportunity at love. A chance at real, lifelong happiness. I'm *not* going to cancel this trip because you or anyone else seems to think it might affect them in some made-up negative way. I'm sorry you came all this way for nothing. Now, if you will excuse me..." She pushed past him.

He harrumphed. Something in the sound worked her last nerve. She turned. "Oh, and another thing. I'll thank you not to call my clients dumb. Every one of those women is smart and well-educated."

"Oh *really?* I couldn't tell from Miss Super out there."

She felt her lips go thin. "Poppy is a smart and interesting woman. All my ladies are."

"Are you implying the men in our town are not well-educated?" He took a step forward, then another, and his body pressed into hers. The rock-hard abs under the deceptively squashy-looking flannel pushed into the softness of her breasts. She gulped. Butterflies danced in her stomach. This was one manly male. Too bad he was so dead set against her company and its plans for Smithfield. He could be one hot poster boy to advertise the wilds of Alaska.

She tipped her head back and stood on tiptoe. It brought her exactly one half inch closer to the bottom of his chin. So much for trying to gain some kind of height advantage on this giant. "No, the men in your town are smart. You, however, are a pushy, overbearing sycophant in desperate need of an education."

He leaned down. "'*Frailty, thy name is woman.*' Don't look so shocked, Miss Cuthbert. All pushy, overbearing sycophants attend good colleges and read Shakespeare. Mine was Harvard. Perhaps you've heard of it?" He took both of her shoulders in his hands and moved her to the right, clearing a path to the door.

"Pardon me. I'm not a toy to be pushed around, *Mr. Mayor.*"

He bent forward, his voice low. "Don't cross me, Miss Cuthbert. I'm not a man who likes to be bested. Just cancel your trip, or find another town. The men of Smithfield are off limits to you and your desperate nymphomaniacs."

"Why, because you want the men all for yourself?" Did she say that? She instantly regretted it and opened her mouth to apologize. She never said things like that. He just got her so...

His eyes narrowed. "What are you saying?"

The apology she was about to offer him died in her throat as he placed a hand at the nape of her neck, removed the glasses from her face and brought his lips to hers. The action, quick and deft, took her completely by surprise.

Tingles raced up and down her spine as his mouth stole over hers. The kiss felt brutal, almost punishing. She held her lips still, fought against the tide trying to pull her under, then gave in to the rush. She parted her lips and melted into him. His tongue flicked over her lips and invaded her mouth. He nipped at her mouth teasingly, with lazy movements that mesmerized her. She licked her tongue over his, delicately at first, then with more enthusiasm. His other arm came up, wrapped around her body and drew her tight against him.

Her breasts pressed to his chest, she leaned in to make more intimate contact with his hard body. God, this felt so good, so...sexy. All internal arguments drained away and she blatantly pushed her belly into his growing erection.

He pulled back. Bent over in his arms, she blinked up at him. For a moment he looked dazed, then his lips thinned and he brought her upright in one smooth motion.

"I think that should answer any lingering questions regarding my sexuality."

That was it. She'd tried to be civil and rein in her tongue, but the way the man treated her burst her tightly held dam of control. "You're an ass."

"Very professional of you."

She slapped a hand over her mouth. "I'm sorry, but you just made me so damned mad. I never swear. Ever."

What looked like the beginnings of a smile played over his features. Damn, the man was downright stunning when he smiled. "I probably deserved that. I'll be going now. I hope you will keep what I said in mind." The smile vanished as easily as it had come. Once more, his face was shadowed and angry looking.

He walked through the swinging door and out into the large room without a backward glance. *The mayor has left the kitchen.* Frustrated, she followed after him, intent on coming up with one last zinger to hurl in his direction. It must have been the silence in a room she expected to be full of buzzing noise, or maybe the shock that seemed to hang palpable in the air, but something grabbed her attention. At least two dozen pairs of eyes were directed at the door to the kitchen. Mouths gaped open as Dave Wellington snatched up his coat and stalked from the room.

Chastity blushed. They'd heard. All of the women heard the whole stupid exchange. She felt mortified.

Dawn, her assistant, hovered behind her. Chastity shook her head. There was nothing she could say to regain her misplaced dignity. Her shocked employee looked at Chas like she'd grown snakes from her head.

Chastity walked to the corner chair where she'd laid her coat and purse. Grabbing them, she turned to Dawn with as much cool as she could muster. "Thanks for everything. If you would, please pack up my laptop and hang on to it over the weekend for me. I'll see you Monday."

Good, at least her voice didn't shake like her insides. She pulled her coat over her shoulders and headed to the front door of the recreation center. Hopefully she'd be able to hail a cab, that or maybe the earth would open up and swallow her. Now that sounded like a plan.

Chapter Two

Cold rain pelted Dave as he headed to the taxi stand. He popped open his umbrella and strode up the sidewalk. *Shit.* Why did he even bother to come all this way? Chastity Cuthbert was one stubborn lady. *Stunning, though.* He frowned. Yes, she was gorgeous, but too much trouble to bother with. With a snort of disgust, he fought the urge to shift his semi-erect cock in his pants. The kiss had shocked him. His lips still burned. He'd meant it as a lesson to her, but it had quickly built into something more.

What the hell happened back there? He tried to sort it all out, but Chastity's face kept swimming before him. Her huge eyes, soft skin, the way her ass felt in his hands. Shaking himself, he held out his hand in the direction of the yellow taxi lights. The cab inched forward.

Reaching for the door handle, Dave looked back in the direction he'd come. A bedraggled and irritated Chastity was hot on his heels. Without an umbrella, she was soaked through. While he watched, she stopped, pulled the pins from her hair and let it drop down her back. It hung longer than he'd expected. Wet tendrils wrapped the sides of her face, showcasing her delicate features. Finally at the cab stand, she looked at him, then pointedly turned her back.

The cold rain rapidly became an icy wash. The streets shone in the lamplights, and the cab's windows took on a sheen that could only come from sleet. Great. You'd think the lower forty-eight would have tame winters in comparison to Alaska, but Dave rarely saw this kind of ice in the north.

He cleared his throat. "Would you like to share a cab?"

She shook her head. "No thank you. There'll be another cab along soon."

Stubborn. Dave fought back a smile. "You're a horrible liar. Get in. I won't bite." The urge to say, *not hard*, washed over him and he gave in to the smile.

Once more her head shook. This time frozen strands of hair smacked her in the jaw. He winced for her. "Really, I'm fine." She peered into the warmth of the cab and her face took on a longing look.

"I'd be happy to call a truce for the duration of the ride." He'd kept his voice low and soft. Almost like he spoke to a scared animal.

She looked up at him, eyes huge. "Are you sure?"

He reached out and touched her cheek, then traced his fingers along her jaw. He wasn't sure if her tremble was from the cold or his touch. She captured her lower lip between pearly teeth and nibbled. He wanted to pull her tight to him, but held back. He didn't want to scare her.

"I don't want to read in tomorrow's paper that you died of exposure Please get in the cab, Chastity."

A sploosh of icy liquid dropped onto the top of her head and rushed down her face. With a defeated sniff, she nodded. "Okay."

A feeling like joy bubbled **up in** Dave at her acquiescence. He did feel like he'd won. **Helping her** into the car, he quickly headed to the other door and **climbed** in.

"Where to?"

Dave gestured to Chastity to give the driver her address.

"You got the cab, you go first."

"Sounds fair enough." He leaned forward and his thigh brushed hers. Sizzling heat replaced the ice cold he'd felt. The warmth traveled up his leg to settle in the region of his cock and happily tortured him. Chastity pulled her leg away, crossed her arms and stared out the window, but not before he caught the startled shock of awareness in her eyes. So, she felt it too. For some reason, this made him feel good, darn good. At least he wasn't the only dope on the planet. Attracted to a woman who wanted to ruin his life.

"Park Hyatt."

"That's a nice hotel." Her voice was soft, but held an edge. Like she'd not really let her guard down.

"Huh?"

She cleared her throat. "The Park Hyatt. It's newly renovated."

What the hell was she up to now? Making small talk? "You live around here?"

"Not far from your hotel, actually." She turned away again. The sudden frost in the cab rivaled what was going on outside.

Dave shrugged. Normal conversation with this woman was a lost cause. It was a shame they hadn't met another way, in any other circumstance.

"I'm sorry you came all this way for nothing."

"I didn't. I told you that I would stop you, and I meant it."

She faced him now. Even in the half light of the streetlights he could see her confusion. Her mouth formed the shape of an O, and she sucked in a breath. "Of all the..." Her small hands balled into fists. "Look, you're the mayor, not the owner of the town. Those men want us there and my ladies paid good money to visit—"

He didn't know why he did it. Didn't even think about it, not really, just went on instinct. Dave leaned forward and kissed her.

She pulled away. "What do you think you're doing?"

He ran a hand though his hair. "I don't know. It seems to shut you up."

"Of all the arrogant, irritating—"

Fingers traced the skin of her cheek. Soft, so incredibly soft. How could someone so beautiful be such a damn pain in the ass?

His hand slipped around to the nape of her neck and pulled her close. For a moment her eyes went wide, but she didn't speak. Trembling, she leaned in, their mouths meeting.

Gently, he sucked her lower lip and nibbled on the delicate skin. She smelled like flowers, light, spring-like. Her body, all curves and softness, fit against his like it was meant to be there.

He should end this. She represented everything he hated about women, but she deepened the contact, turning his will to mush. She tangled her tongue with his in an erotic dance that drained the blood from every place in his body. Every place but his cock. Turgid and ready, it strained between them. She shivered in his arms and he drew her sexy little body onto his lap.

The cab came to a wobbly stop. Their mouths parted and she looked up at him with a gasp. He too felt like the breath had been sucked from his body. The red stoplight above them was blurred by the ice on the windows. It turned from red to green. Beneath them, the cab's tires spun uselessly on the pavement as the ice made it almost impossible to accelerate.

The cabdriver swore as the engine revved and the tires fought for purchase on the slick street beneath them. Inching along, they finally came to a stop in front of his hotel. Chastity slid off his lap.

Dave looked at the woman next to him. He shouldn't want her, shouldn't be drawn to her. The V of her shirt showed a hint of breast and he swallowed, hard. "Come with me."

Where the hell had that come from? He opened his mouth to take it back, when she turned to face him and licked a pink tongue over her lips. Dave's heart skipped a beat.

"Sorry, folks. This is the end of the line. I'm not risking it out there till they salt the roads."

She glanced up at the cabbie, and back at Dave, confusion clear on her face. "I don't think that's a good idea. I can walk from here. Thank you very much."

Dave looked around. Iced over, the sidewalks appeared more than treacherous. "You're not going to walk in this."

Her head came up, the fight back in her eyes. "Don't tell me what I can and cannot do. I've been taking care of myself for a long time and—"

Dave placed a hand over her mouth. Her eyes narrowed, but she went silent. "I don't know why I'm so attracted to you. I should spank you. I think the attraction's mutual. I don't want to fight right now. I want to take you to my room and make love to you. What do you want?"

Reluctantly, he pulled his hand away and waited for an answer.

Lip between her teeth, she turned her head to him, then up the street. "Caught between the devil and the deep blue sea."

"The devil? Am I really so bad?" It came out almost a whisper.

The indecision was clear on her face. "If I do this, and I'm not saying I'm going to, that does not mean I'm giving in. The Alaskan Connection has a signed contract and we're coming, like it or not. This is just animal attraction, plain and simple. Nothing more. Agreed?"

"Agreed." Something in Dave released and he felt like howling into the moonless night.

Dave grasped her hand, afraid she would pull away, and helped her from the cab and into the lobby. He barely noticed the warm wood tones and masculine feel of the lobby he'd been so impressed with earlier in the day. He was bringing a woman to his room, Chastity Cuthbert no less. Pressing the up button at the elevator, Dave leaned in and kissed her once more.

His fingers wrapped in her hair, and he pulled her close with a groan. The elevator doors whooshed open and somehow they moved inside. It felt like all the passion of their ongoing fight was in her mouth and tongue. The touch of her mouth against his felt unbelievable.

"Oh God." Her needy moan ripped straight through his body in a way he'd not expected. The elevator came to a halt, the doors whispering open. She looked up with a dazed expression and laughed.

He smiled in return. "I think we're supposed to get off the elevator now."

She nodded. "Yep, I think that's what we're supposed to do."

Hand in hand, they headed to his door. Impatiently, he hunted for the keycard, jammed it in the lock and twisted the door handle.

Her arms wrapped around his waist and they fell into the room, onto the floor, Dave's body cushioning their fall. Twisting around, he captured the shell of her ear with his lips. Nipping at her ear, he held her wriggling body against him.

She felt soft and sexy and full of desire in his arms. She left no questions about what she wanted. Good. Dave hated games.

"Let's get out of these wet clothes." Her throaty voice made him harder, if that was possible. Passion filled her gaze. There was no hesitation at all. She wanted this as much as he did. No teasing, just yearning. Standing, she unbuttoned her coat and dropped it in the entryway behind her. Her suit jacket and skirt followed. Her fingers toyed with, then fumbled over the buttons on her shirt.

Nerves. She's as nervous as I am. Something about the tension in the line of her body surprised and touched him. A look of frustration crossed her beautiful face. He rose and placed his hands on her shoulders, massaging gently. Slowly they moved down, brushing the tops of her breasts through the cloth of her shirt, until they reached the small pearl-colored buttons.

Tenderly, he undid each one, bottom to top. When her hands covered his, he paused at the button over her bra. Did she want him to stop?

Pulling his hands, she popped the button off the fabric.

Lips curving in a playful, kittenish way, she grabbed his jacket and yanked it down his arms. Buttons flying, his shirt followed hers.

Now this is more like it.

Pushing him to the ground, she straddled his body. With a sly smile, she unhooked her bra, yanked it from her body and dropped it to the floor. He sucked in an appreciative breath. Her breasts, now free, were stunning. Large, but beautifully shaped. Perfect for his hands to cover. His thumbs moved over her nipples, flicking them gently, while she wriggled seductively against his cock. Letting out a needy moan, he pushed against her. She felt amazing against his body. Warm and willing.

With a laugh, he flipped her on her back and ran his fingers over the mound of her panties, playing along her slit. She lifted her hips and he pulled her panties from her in one movement.

Naked under him, she looked like a sexy angel. With a shiver, he placed one, then two fingers inside her and slowly fucked her with them. Her eyes closed ecstatically.

"You're so beautiful. Do you like this? Do you want more?"

She moaned. That was it. He either took her or came in his pants like a teenager. Standing, he removed his pants and shorts as fast as possible, adding them to the thick pile of discarded clothes.

Pushing herself to her elbows, she watched him get naked, her gaze hungry.

Gorgeous. It was the only word to describe Chastity. Her body pale, but not too white, the sheen and color of well-worn pearls. Legs, long for such a petite frame. He'd heard the young kids in Smithfield refer to some of the tourists as hot. He never got that, before tonight. Chastity Cuthbert was hot. *Smokin'.*

Holding out his hand to her, he helped her to her feet, picked her up in his arms and carried her to the bed. He dropped her in the middle of the mattress. She let out a laugh and held her arms out to him. Never let it be said Dave Wellington had to be invited twice. He grinned, crawled up on the bed and hovered over her, supporting himself with his arms. His mouth came down on hers in a quick kiss, and he leaned over the end of the bed and reached into the suitcase on the stand. Fishing around, he pulled a condom out.

Ripping the foil open, he leaned back and pumped his cock a few times.

Chastity stared. Dave fought back an evil grin. He wasn't exactly a monster, but still, he was comfortable with his size and girth.

She rose to her knees, bent down and drew the tip of his cock into her warm mouth.

Smile gone, he sucked the breath in with a hiss. Moving her hair out of the way, she leaned in and licked him, base to tip. The feeling of her tongue on his cock made it jump in need. Her hand encircled the base as her velvet-soft mouth washed the length of him. He moaned. Her hot mouth on his shaft felt incredible. He watched, glassy eyed, as her cheeks hollowed from the force of her suck.

She pulled back and held out her hand. Dave just stared dumbly at it.

"The condom..."

"Duh." He placed it in her outstretched hand with a sheepish grin.

With two hands, she rolled it down over him.

"That's a neat little feat. Should I ask where you learned it?"

"Eighth grade."

His brows knit. "Isn't that a little young?"

Her laughter rang like bells. "It was a dare at a party. I used a banana."

"Lucky banana."

She guided herself onto the tip of his waiting cock. Pushing down, she impaled herself on him with a gasp.

God she was incredible.

His hips pressed into her and withdrew gently. Forcing herself down, she filled herself with him again. She was incredibly greedy and he loved it. *Here's hoping you don't come on the third stroke.* Maybe he should think about bricks, or being chased by lions. Anything but this incredibly sexy woman fucking him senseless.

He pulled her ear to his mouth. "Careful, sweetheart, or I'll think you want it hard and wild."

She moved her hips suggestively.

"Okay, pretty lady, you get what you asked for."

"Bring it on, wild man."

His thigh trapped hers and he flipped her onto her back, forcing his cock to the hilt, withdrawing and pounding into her again.

She moaned and wrapped her legs around him, meeting him thrust for thrust.

Their gazes caught and held. He felt orgasm build at the back of his mind until it rolled over his body in wave after wave of mind-bending pleasure.

With a gasp, her head dropped back, her fingernails bit into his shoulder and she began to shake beneath him.

Spent, he held her close, kissing her along her ear and neck. Something about the closeness felt intimate in a way that Dave didn't expect, but welcomed. He didn't want to analyze this moment now. He didn't have the energy. Besides, he was sick of worrying about women and their motives. He brushed the hair from her face as she sleepily snuggled down against his body. It felt good and right and he'd worry about tomorrow later.

"You bring out the passion in me, Chastity Cuthbert. I want to get to know you better. I'm in town for a few more days. Will you stay with me?"

She stiffened, then nodded. It felt reluctant, but the warmth of her body against his lulled him. Her body relaxed and he let go and drifted into a dreamless sleep.

ℂ

Dave reached out. There was something off, but he couldn't put his finger on it. He moved. Sore, his hips were sore. Memory flooded back. The argument, Chastity bedraggled but sexy as hell in the cab. Her open willing face as he made love to her.

With a smile, he opened his eyes. To an empty pillow.

Confused, he stood and looked around the room. His clothes lay in a heap on the floor, but her things were gone. He stalked over to the pile and frowned. Nothing. No evidence that she'd even been here. A dull gleam caught his eye and he bent down to investigate. The button from her blouse. The one that flew off when she pulled his hands apart and exposed her bra. He picked it up and stared at it.

"Well, Cinderella left the ball, but she left something behind."

Angry, he balled his fist around the mother of pearl, then dropped his hand to his side, drained of all energy. With a snort of indifference, he grabbed his clothes and began to pack with his free hand, tossing clothes into his open suitcase. If that was how she wanted to play it, then fine by him. He'd fly home early and stop her business dead in its tracks.

Hand open, he looked once more at the button, then placed it carefully in the zippered pocket on the side of his suitcase. At least he'd have a reminder of his stupidity, *and Chastity.* He ignored his inner voice as he headed to the shower.

Chapter Three

"Here, drink this. You'll feel better."

Chastity took a sip from the cup Freddie handed her. It burned all the way down and she coughed uncontrollably, while Freddie pounded on her back.

"Dear God, what is this? I thought you said it was tea?" She furrowed her brow accusingly.

"It is tea." He looked sheepish. "With a little Jack Daniels thrown in for good measure." He flopped down on the couch, adjusted a lighted mirror on the coffee table, opened a plastic box and removed one black spiky object with the tip of a finger. "So, tell me what happened next."

"I screwed him and then I ran away with my tail between my legs."

Finger to his eye, he stopped, pulled the false eyelash back and stared at her. "Oh no you did not."

She sucked in another swallow of Freddie's tea. It burned just as badly as before, but this time she didn't cough. "Oh yes I did."

Freddie stood and applauded, the lash on the end of his finger waving in the air as he did so. "Well good for you, screwing Mr. Big and Beefy. I'm proud of you. Woman power and all that Helen Reddy shit."

"I'm in shock."

"That I applauded?"

"Nope, that you know who Helen Reddy is. I thought you only worshipped Barbra and Liza."

"Honey, I'm a cliché transvestite, but not a total cliché transvestite. I am woman, hear me roar." He stopped, his mouth opened in an O and he began to applaud again and jump up and down like an excited three-year-old. "Oh my God! I love you!" He bent down and pressed a kiss to her forehead. "I can put that into my act. Why the hell didn't I think of that before? It's a scream. I can see it now. 'Freddie Fabulous Sings for Feminine Emancipation'. Don't you just love it?"

She smiled. "Actually, I do. I'd come to see that every night for a week."

He waved his hand in the air and sat back down. "You always come to see my act. You're more reliable than my parents. Speaking of whom, they send their love and lots of frou-frou air kisses."

"How are Mabel and Ned?"

"Oh, you know, off on another cruise. This time to India. They swore to bring me back a fabulous sari."

She sucked in another mouthful of the drink. She had to hand it to her friend. The thing became less nasty as you drank it. "You must have the coolest parents in the world."

He'd gone back to placing his eyelash. She watched him carefully line it up with his lid and press it in place. "There, perfection. Oh and to answer your question, sure do. They always wanted a daughter. With five boys, they were almost relieved when one of them turned to the dark side. So, what's this animal's name? Mayor somebody or other."

"Dave Wellington."

"Like the boot?" He laughed. That's one of the things Chastity loved about Freddie. He had a strong sense of the ridiculous.

"Yep, just like the boot."

"Well, good for you for going for what you want. A year ago you would have run home to your vibrator, boo-hooing all the way."

He stood and sashayed to his closet. Chastity smiled. Freddie's studied movements were more feminine than any woman she'd ever known. Too bad more of it didn't rub off on her. They'd been friends for five years, since she'd moved to Chicago and the small apartment where Milwaukee, Ashland and Division met. All alone, she'd initially been afraid of the six-foot drag queen, but he turned on the charm, pulled her under his wing and fussed over her. Chastity loved it. Since her parents died in a car wreck when she was in college, she'd been alone. Freddie made a great big sister.

"So, dahling, what are you going to do about Mr. Big and Beefy Alaska?"

She shrugged. "What can I do? Maybe I'll see him this summer and... I have too much riding on this to change now. Even if I am terrified of running into him again. Besides, summer in Alaska is one of those things that cleanses my soul. I'm not giving it up because I had hot and dirty sex with a stranger." She leaned forward, set the cup on the coffee table and placed her chin in her hands. "I don't get it though. Why did I run away? What scared me so much?"

"Hard to say, maybe he really did something to you and you were afraid of getting hurt? What do you think of this frock?"

She shook her head. "Too busy. I don't know why you bought that one. Grab the plum. You never wear it and it's fantastic on you. Highlights your long legs and hides your pitifully flat chest."

He tossed a silk-covered hanger at her. She ducked easily and laughed.

"Poo, just cause you're blessed with an overabundance of boobbie-liciousness. Have some of it cut off and put on me. Lord knows you've got it to spare."

She cupped her breasts, squeezed, then fell back on the couch giggling. The booze was getting to her. "Yea, well, fat lot of good these have done me. Do you see a line-up of men? I don't." Her mind wandered back to the night before and the hot man asleep on the hotel bed. Nope, she couldn't go back now.

"Knocked your bobby socks right off, did he?"

She nodded.

He grabbed the plum dress, walked to the floor-to-ceiling mirror and held it up. "You know, this does seem to do something for me. How the hell do you manage it? You dress like a librarian and you dress me like a dream. I'd say it was unfair, if it didn't benefit me so much."

"I don't know. I just suck at dressing myself."

"Well, at least you let your hair down. You look positively eighteen twenty-three when it's up."

She reached back. Used to it up, the feeling of it resting against her back was almost erotic. "I wear it that way to look older, so the clients will respect me."

"Oh la-de-da, the clients. Can't have them think of you as any sort of competition now, can we? Nonsense. You're a woman. Dress like one." He plopped next to her. "Look, just try this. Go to Alaska this summer with a few new pairs of jeans, your hair down and some reasonably sexy T-shirts. Can you manage that?"

Chas shrugged. "I don't know what good you think it will do, but yeah, I can do that." She stood. "I better go, you'll be late." She bent down and kissed him on the cheek. "Break a leg, sweetie. I've got to try to get some sleep."

He laughed. "Saturday night's show's a breeze. The audience is all drunk. Catch you tomorrow for din-din?"

"Yep." She yawned. "I'm making Chicken Vesuvio. You coming alone, or with a date?"

"Alone. I'm single for the entire month of April. I'll screw around again in May."

"You and your weird schedules. Love ya. Mean it."

"Right back atcha, honey-cakes. Silly little air kisses and dogs that fit in your purse to you too."

She made her way over discarded gowns, six-inch heels and various makeup cases to the door.

Crossing the hallway, she pushed the door to her apartment open. The stale smell of old air met her. She closed the door shut behind her, hit the light switch and dropped her keys on the counter. Clean to the point of being pristine, her apartment felt sterile and unloved. Furnished from a package sold by the local high-end decorator du jour, it lacked warmth.

Wandering into her bathroom, she pulled the rumpled white shirt from her navy skirt and tossed it on the floor. She glanced down at it and sighed in frustration. Scooping it up, she dropped it into the hamper. She admired Freddie's mess. It spoke of his wonderfully spontaneous life. Staring into the mirror, she brushed her hair out. It fell in brown whirls around her shoulders and halfway down her back. Removing her glasses, she stared at the face that peered back at her. For thirty-one, she looked okay. No lines, no wrinkles and her skin was finally clear of the acne so bad she'd been called Spots in school. Still, she wasn't exactly gorgeous either. *Bor-ing.* She

101

finished undressing and grabbed her nightgown from the hook on the back of the door.

A few steps had her in the bedroom. Without flipping on the light, she crawled to the headboard and gazed out at downtown Chicago. The city twinkled. She'd been so happy to move here. To leave the pain of her parents' deaths behind. She loved it, at first. Now the air seemed to press down on her with smog so thick she could feel it when she breathed. The EL, once so amazing to her, now just another crowded way to get from point A to point B. She longed for...what?

She blew air out. Her lips felt bruised and sore. She ran her fingers across them, remembering Dave's kiss and his body moving against hers. Was this what her life had come to? Holding fast to memories of a hasty mistake made by a man she was afraid to see again? She punched her pillow and lay down, willing her mind to shut off and let her sleep.

Images of Dave Wellington's strong face and stunning body swam in her half dreams. She rolled over and sat up. The man was in her head and she wanted him out. *You're a horrible liar. You want to go back there and molest him some more.*

The clock on top of the TV flashed the time, eleven fifty-nine, then midnight. April first. April Fools' Day. Well, that man had certainly made a fool out of her. So what? So what if she responded to his touch, begged for him to take her? She'd forget all about him by the time she took her party to Alaska in June. Sure, Smithfield was a small town, but she could avoid him. Alaska was a big state. She'd only be there for a week. Besides, there were ten men to one woman in Smithfield. Maybe it was time for Chastity Cuthbert to meet an Alaskan hunk of her own?

With that thought, she lay her head back down and finally began to fall asleep. Her own Alaskan man. She tried to ignore the forest green eyes that seemed to mock her half-formed plans.

Chapter Four

"Oh shit."

Chastity looked up at her home for the next week—the Lazy Fish motel in Smithfield, Alaska—and her mouth dropped open. One half of the hotel's roof was caved in.

"Now, don't you worry, Miss Cuthbert. We have alternate plans."

Chastity faced Smithfield's deputy mayor, William Pierce-Prince—or Bill as he'd asked her to call him when he'd picked her up at the airport. "Um, how long has this been like this?"

"Oh, it happened over the winter. We didn't want to alarm you none. We thought it would be fixed by now, but the cruise ship shows keep us all pretty busy 'round here."

"But what about my clients?"

"Don't you worry about them. We still have fifty good rooms here and we got rooms at the married couples' homes for the rest of the women, excepting you."

"Where am I going to stay?"

"Oh, we got a place for you. Our esteemed mayor is off on a fishing trip. So we figured it would only be neighborly of him if you stayed at his place."

She turned to Bill, eyes wide. "You mean you're going to put me up in the house of a man who does not want me here and not tell him about it?"

He grinned. "Don't worry on it. I'll escort you to your digs and the rest of the boys here will meet the ladies coming in. They're mighty excited about the ladies, but don't expect too much. In Alaska the odds are good, but the goods are odd." He chuckled. "Can't wait till the dance tonight. You should see the town hall. It looks mighty pretty."

She smiled. "I'm sure it's lovely, but about using Dave Wellington's house…"

He held up his hand. "Nope, don't want to hear nothing 'bout it. Dave's a fair man and he'd not want you sleeping in the cold. Don't know as you can tell, but houses round here are pretty small. Built up on flat places on the hillsides. We did what we could, it's important that you ladies have a nice warm bed, with privacy. Don't want to shove you in with a bunch of desperate bachelors."

Just then, a high-pitched giggle sounded above the crowd. Poppy. William cocked his ear to listen.

"Although, seems like maybe some of your ladies would enjoy that sort of thing."

Chas laughed. "Seems like you may be right."

He gestured with his arm. "After you."

"Um, my things…"

"Don't you worry 'bout them none. The men will bring 'em by later. Won't hurt them one bit to do some real work. All that fake mining and acting for the tourists turns 'em soft."

Chas raised an eyebrow. "So, I take it you aren't keen on the changing of the guard around here?"

"Bah, you mean that crap Dave's putting on? Nope, it's not what real men do. Still, since the closing of the mine, it's the best we've got. His cabin's just up this road a piece."

Chastity looked down. The "road" Bill referred to was nothing more than a dirt two-track. "Aren't the ships bringing jobs to the town?"

"Yep, good ones. We almost can't keep up. That's why we're pinning so much hope on you and your lady Cheechakos. We need to settle these Wild West types down. Start a few new families. We've lost some, we'll lose some more, if we lose too many..."

They'd been steadily climbing the entire time they'd been walking. Now Bill turned and looked back, Chastity followed. The view almost took her breath away. Below her, peeking through the trees, was the town of Smithfield. The buildings, all made of logs and timber, gave it a feel she'd only found in Alaska. Beyond the trees was the inside passage, beyond that, more tree-covered islands.

"Where's the dock?"

Bill waved his arm to the right. Through the trees, a long stretch of concrete laid out in the water, like a pier.

He took off his hat and rubbed his head. "I don't like the changes the big ships bring. Three thousand people at a pop coming in here, taking over the town. All wanting crap souvenirs and bitching 'cause they don't see bears in the middle of the street. What kind of town has bears in the middle of the street?"

She laughed. "I don't know, but I'm pretty sure I don't want to find out."

He continued walking. In a few more steps they came to a clearing with a neat log cabin in the middle. Small by any standards, it held the charm only a cabin in the Alaskan woods

106

could. Wildflowers filled the meadow-like area in front of the house. A small garden, sprouts barely out of the ground, stood off to one side. She wanted to look around, but Bill was making his way to the door.

"Isn't it locked?"

"Nobody locks up around here. It's an island." He pushed the door open and held it for her. "Here ya go. Your humble abode."

Cautiously, she entered and looked around. The inside was as small as the outside promised. One wall held a sink, oven and refrigerator. A large table, covered in a red-checked cloth, sat near the kitchen. To her left was what passed for the living room. A couch, comfortable chair and a coffee table sat in front of what looked like a well-used fireplace, filled bookshelves on either side.

"Ain't much, but it's comfortable. Bedroom's through there." He nodded at a door. "Bath's next to it and that door's his office. Pretty plain, Alaska cabins are, but it serves Dave well. Speaking of him..." Bill cleared his throat. "He don't mean to be so inhospitable. He's just... Well, it's hard for him, all you women. Hurts his heart."

She knit her brow. "I thought we were a bunch of sirens here to steal the menfolk. How does that hurt his heart?"

"Begging your pardon for gossiping, but you oughta know the truth. He has a brother who met some gal on the internet. She came up here, hated it and broke the poor man's heart. Kid bought a homestead near Fairbanks and won't even talk to Dave anymore. Blames him. Seems the woman compared Tad to Dave a lot and Tad always came up short. Tad blames Dave and Dave blames women in general." He looked at the door. "Well, if you won't be needing me, I'm gonna head over to the town hall to finish setting up for the dance."

Wandering over to the bookshelves, she looked back and nodded.

"Good. I expect you'll find your way to the hall. Straight down Dave's road, make a right. Hall's on your left as you enter town. Don't blink, you'll miss it. Eight on the nose."

"Sure thing, Bill." Still caught up in the books, she nodded again and heard the door close behind her. She hunted through the books for one in particular. Then she saw it. "Damn." The complete works of William Shakespeare. She stuck her tongue out at the book and turned to check out the rest of the cabin.

The door to the bedroom swung open easily. Larger than she thought it would be, the room smelled of dark wood and Dave. Sunlight filled the room, lighting on warm cherry furniture and soft muted colors of the linens. She ran her hand over the bedpost. It appeared to be hand carved with leaves and vines climbing the sides. The bed, dressing table and side tables were smooth as polished glass. A framed photo caught her eye. A smiling Dave, fish held triumphantly in both hands, stood next to a sober-looking man whose eyes resembled Dave's too much to be a coincidence. This must be Tad, his brother. She was glad Bill took the time to explain Dave a little better. The sad story made him seem like less of an ass. Her gaze caught the green of his eyes and her stomach lurched. She ran a finger over his face. She missed him. How could she possibly miss someone she'd been with for only a few hours? Even if they did... She blushed.

She put the photo down and headed to the bathroom. A large soaking tub, along with a gorgeous pedestal sink and marble on the floors, stood in complete contrast to the rest of the cabin. A quick poke into Dave's office was met with a mélange of papers piled high on every surface. Closing the door, she turned to the kitchen, her tummy rumbling.

Ugh, food. How long had it been since she'd eaten? Too long. She wandered to the cupboard and pulled out a can of soup.

"Well, Dave, I sure hope you aren't saving this for a special occasion." He sure was going to be mad when he found out that his home harbored the head jezebel of The Alaskan Connection and woman who'd snuck out like a thief in the night from his hotel room. She shivered. She planned to be long gone by the time he got back.

Chapter Five

Chastity forced herself up the hill. The day had been an unqualified success. The ladies were thrilled with the men they'd met and the men seemed equally enamored. Everyone had found someone, everyone but her. She'd worn her tight jeans and pretty tops. She chatted animatedly with everyone, but no one struck her fancy. *That's 'cause you're hung up on the one Smithfield resident who's out of town.* She told her brain to shut up.

The cabin loomed before her. It was eleven o'clock at night, but the sun had just set a half an hour earlier, leaving the world in perpetual twilight. It would rise again at three-forty-five in the morning. The world seemed magical in the half dark, like fairies could come out and dance in the spaces between the trees.

Dismissing her imaginings, she dragged her tired self into the bedroom, pulling clothes off as she walked. She left her undies on and crawled into the soft bed. Ah, heaven. Dave Wellington was a jerk, but a jerk with a heavenly bedroom.

She snuggled down and took in a deep whiff. Her eyes opened. The pillow, even in his absence, smelled of the woods, musk and soap, a smell that was uniquely Dave's. She sat up, the memory of hot sex vivid in her mind. The smell drew her mind back to that night and the feelings that washed over her body when he held her against him and sweetly assaulted her body with his.

Thinking about the sex brought heat to her face, but liquid warmth to her center. God, he was sexy as hell. Why fight it anymore? She wanted him again, so what? She also wanted to screw Brad Pitt. That didn't mean he was any more for her than Dave Wellington was.

ᘒ

Damn. He blinked hard and rubbed his eyes with his free hand. They didn't want to stay open anymore. He was about to lose the battle to stay awake. Served him right, heading home in the middle of the night. "I'm an idiot." Dave Wellington ignored the little voice that whispered to him that he'd packed up his fishing gear and headed back for more than some belated intervention with the town's men.

The tall pines on either side of the road loomed in the dark, like furry sentinels that blocked his peripheral vision. Normally they made a cozy tunnel to drive through. Now the sameness of the darkened scenery closed in on him, making sleep look all the better.

Finally, the opening to the double track that led from the main road to his cabin came into view. He turned the wheel left and shot gravel from the back of his tires. Home sounded too heavenly to take his time.

He pulled up to the house, pushed open the car door and shoved it closed behind him with his boot. It was good to be home. A warm glow in the windows caught his eye. He wrinkled his brow. He didn't remember leaving a light on. He shrugged. Bill stopped by and raided his fridge on a regular basis. He'd probably forgotten the light. Dave hoped his old friend had

111

remembered to close the door, unlike a year ago. Nothing like a bear shitting on your living room floor to welcome you home after a long trip.

He tested the door. Good, latch tight. No bears this time. Walking into the cabin, he switched off the living room light, but not before catching a glimpse of his sink and the clean dishes stacked neatly beside it. Bill never bothered to wash a dish after a raid. The guy was getting daft in his old age.

"Someone's been eating *my* porridge."

He chuckled. The bear memory brought out the bad jokes in him. He shrugged out of his jacket, pulled off his shirt and un-buttoned his fly. Opening his bedroom door to pitch black, he kicked off his boots and shucked his jeans.

What was that?

A deeply drawn breath stopped him in his tracks. Shit, maybe a bear had managed to get into his house. He fumbled for the light switch and flicked it on.

He looked at the bed and blinked, trying to make sense of the view. There, practically naked, lay the reason for his stress. Chastity Cuthbert snoring away, oblivious to his presence. *What the hell?* Well, well, this was an interesting turn of events. He flicked the light off and on a few times to rouse her. She didn't so much as move a muscle. Were it not for the loud breathing he'd wonder if she were alive.

She lay on her side, long reddish-brown hair spread out behind her, mouth slightly open, breasts moving with her breath and her ass round and full in her panties... Damn, his cock rose, along with his irritation. What was it about this woman that made him both pant like a dog in heat and want to take her over his knee? At that thought his cock jumped. *Down, boy. She's not for you. She left you in the middle of the night.*

She snorted and rolled over. One breast popped free of the sheet. The large perfect globe moved tantalizingly with each inhalation. He gaped. Damn, he was invading her privacy in all kinds of unforgivable ways, but the sight of that perfect pink-tipped mound turned his brain to mush and rooted him in place as if she'd tied him there.

See, this is exactly why you didn't want these women up here in the first place. They rob you of your focus.

Yeah, what the hell was she doing, mostly naked in *his* house? He crossed his arms, leaned against the doorjamb and took a breath. "Someone's been sleeping in my bed, and that someone's still here."

Chapter Six

Chastity's brain crawled grumpily out of the fog of sleep. She blinked her eyes open and held an arm up to ward off the light from the ceiling fixture. Had she fallen asleep with it on? No, she vaguely remembered collapsing in the dark. She sat up and looked around the room. Everything seemed just as she remembered it, everything but the mostly naked man lounging casually against the wall, enormous bulge in his undershorts.

"What the *hell* are you doing here?"

"Enjoying the view." His gaze moved lazily over her body, leaving liquid heat behind.

She glanced down. "Oh my gosh." Grabbing the edge of the sheet, she pulled it over her. She swallowed her embarrassment and looked him in the eye. Smug. That was the only word to describe his face. She raked a gaze pointedly up and down his mostly naked form. She intended the glance to be dismissive, but she lingered a bit longer than necessary on the amazing-looking protuberance in his shorts. *Maybe he didn't notice.* Unbelievably, it grew even larger. *Damn, he noticed.*

Drawing her legs beneath her, she rolled to her knees. Good, she felt less vulnerable. "Bill told me you went fishing." She'd not meant to affect such a snotty tone, but the nearly naked man by the door dragged it out of her.

"Let's just say I was not comfortable leaving my town to your ministrations and came home early. To my home, which you're in I might add."

She lifted her chin. "Bill told me it would be okay."

"Bill talks out his ass."

"Fine then, if you'll just leave the room, I'll pack my things and go."

"By go, I hope you mean home."

She lifted her chin a bit higher. "No, go sleep somewhere else. I'm not leaving Smithfield. You can't make me." *So there, neener, neener, neener.* Her teeth clamped down on her lower lip. She sounded like a dork. Something that happened far too much around this man.

He waved a hand. "Forget it. You can stay. Bill's an ass, but not a complete ass. He didn't expect me to be home. The town's full. When he finds out, he's gonna have a good laugh. Far be it for me to wreck his day."

She narrowed her eyes. "Oh, no. There's no way I'm staying uninvited."

The wide, strong shoulders lifted and sank with surprising elegance. "It's up to you, but you're welcome to my bed."

She felt her pussy tighten and her panties become damp. *Oh no, not again. Not this man. Anyone but this man. I am not attracted to him anymore.* Her body seemed to think otherwise, because her stomach filled with the flutters of what felt like a thousand wings. She pulled the sheet closer to her chest and tried to muster something resembling proud dignity.

He turned, displaying his amazing, hard ass, casually grabbed a robe off the door, pulled it on and belted it tight. "It's late. We can't fix this tonight. Just sleep here. I'll go to the couch. I can worry about getting your ass out of here in the morning."

"What? Oh no. You don't call the shots, I do. I'm leaving— tonight!" She tossed her legs over the bed, stood, then bent over and plucked her clothing off the floor. Dropping the sheet, she looked down at exposed boobs, grabbed the edge of the sheet and wrapped it back up. With a huff, she marched to the door to push past him. His hand shot out, grasping her upper arm. The firm yet gentle grip sent her body into overdrive.

"I told you. You can stay here tonight. I meant it. If you're worried about what's left of your virtue, it's safe with me. I wouldn't touch you with a ten-foot pole."

She twisted her arm and gave his hand an evil look. "You seem to be touching me now. I'm leaving."

His mouth came closer. "No, you're not. Go lie down in the bed."

"No. You lie in it. I don't want to. It smells like you anyway."

"And what, exactly, is wrong with that?"

She blushed and shook her head. "Nothing. Just get out of my way."

"No." His voice was softer now, the insistence gone. Something in his gaze mesmerized her. His eyes, so close and so green. How could eyes be that color? Were they contacts? She searched the edge of the mossy soft irises looking for a telltale line. Nothing. She leaned forward a bit.

Her gaze dropped to his full, mobile lips. The anger that filled her earlier evaporated into thin air. She drew in a shaky breath.

"I *insist* you stay." His mouth covered hers.

She should pull away, should at least offer a token resistance. Instead, she melted into his hard body. The smell of sandalwood and pine forests that clung to him enrobed her. His mouth moved against hers in soft seduction, belying the anger she'd heard in his voice.

Powerful arms pulled her body to mould with his. He licked at her lips, rough, then gentle, until she opened her mouth to his assault. The feel of his tongue over hers sent shivers through her body. They met and swirled together, coalescing into color and need in her pussy.

He lifted her and pulled her onto the hardness of his cock. She squirmed to better feel the turgid member, pushing her slit against it through the robe and sheet, wanting more. A finger touched her chin and he leaned back to look into her eyes. His half-lidded gaze seemed to question her intentions.

Oh God, what am I doing? The finger traveled over her chin, down her neck to her collarbone where it toyed with a loose strand of hair there. She gulped and tried to look away but the compelling green eyes seemed to hold her in place. Was this what she wanted, why she didn't insist on staying somewhere else? His hand, now moving seductively over the tops of her breasts, felt wonderful and sensual. It had been so long since she'd been with him, and he set her body on fire. There would be consequences. She could not sneak out of Alaska if this was a mistake. She had a job to do and she'd have to face him for days to come. She buried her head in his shoulder to infuse her mind with his sexy scent and feel.

Screw consequences, they're overrated. Still nervous, she leaned up and placed her lips against his. He didn't move, barely breathed. His mouth rested against hers, waiting. She reached out with her tongue and ran it over his lips. They parted, and she tasted heat, mixed with something that was all Dave. Opening his robe with her free hand, she moved it over his chest muscles. Her fingers found the flat disc of one nipple and flicked it, teasing it to life. He moaned against her mouth. God, he sounded so needy and sexy.

One powerful leg pressed between hers. She parted her legs to rub herself along bare thigh. Her clit was on fire. The need to relieve the ache growing in her belly felt overwhelming. Tearing her lips from his, she licked down the side of his neck. Dave's head dropped back, and his hand moved from her ass to the back of her head. Strong fingers twined in her hair and pulled her into him. The smell of his neck, the rough hands on her hair, the feel of his hard thigh against her pussy seemed like too much. She sucked the skin of his neck and whimpered against him.

Hair released, strong hands roamed down her back and grabbed her ass. He stroked and massaged the globes, then lifted her up. Surprised, she wrapped both of her legs tightly around his torso as he carried her to the bed. He sank to the mattress, Chastity on top of him. Sitting up, she rubbed her soaking pussy over his rock-hard cock in circles. Their gazes met. The half-smile on his face made him look like a naughty little boy. She smiled in return and they both laughed.

"What are we doing?" She bit her lip and waited.

His lips twisted in a sardonic little grin. "Well, if you don't know..."

Narrowing her eyes, she circled her hips once more and listened to his indrawn hiss of breath. "Oh, I know what we're doing. I'm pretty sure I'm about to be thoroughly fucked. What I meant was, will we regret it?"

He shrugged. "Probably, but I'm not sure I can get up and go on if I don't have you tonight. What do you think?"

She shook her head. "Me either. So damn the cost and full steam ahead?"

His hand moved over her face in a tender caress. "Only if you're sure."

"I don't think I am, but I want you."

"Want what?" His voice sounded clogged with need.

Running her hand over his chest, she flicked a finger over one semi-hard nipple. "This. To touch you, taste you..."

"Fuck me?"

Dropping her gaze, she nodded. His hands moved up her torso to her breasts. The fingers of one hand caressed her, then squeezed a nipple between his thumb and forefinger until she gasped and tossed back her head. His free hand moved over the other breast and mimicked the action. A quiver of pain-tinged pleasure washed over her body.

"Do you like that, Chastity?"

She looked away. His fingers tightened until she cried out and rubbed her pussy against him.

"God, you're so beautiful." He brushed his hands over her shoulders. His gaze followed his hands as they roamed over her breasts and down her body to the top of her panties. One finger ran along the edge, against the elastic. "Do you want me to touch you here?"

His honey-thick voice accompanied by the thumb stroking over her vulva drove her wild. She moaned and tried to press her clit against him.

"Say it. Tell me what you want."

Panting, she looked down at him. His sea green gaze seemed to bore into her. She felt shy and almost uncomfortable with her need. She hesitated a moment and his thumb pulled back. This wasn't a man who stood for coy. Why was she being so shy now? Last time... Her mind wandered back to the overwhelming emotions he'd made her experience. "I want you to fuck me."

"With pleasure."

Strong arms wrapped around her, his legs somehow untangled themselves from under her and she found herself on her back beneath him. She blinked up at him. "What the...?"

He grinned. "Wrestled all through high school. Impressed?"

She laughed. "Very. Shakespeare *and* wrestling? It's enough to make a girl weak. So, what next?"

He placed his mouth against the shell of her ear. The hot breath stroking against her skin sent tingles through her. "Now, I taste your sweet pussy."

Her eyes widened. "No, I mean, umm..."

He pulled back, his gaze boring into hers. "Chastity, if you're uncomfortable..."

She shook her head. "It's not that. Well it is, but... No one's ever..."

His eyes narrowed. "Not ever?"

"Nope, not even one time."

"Do you want to do this?"

"Yes."

His hand moved over her panties, then under the delicate fabric, fingers brushing over her hard little clit sending shock waves racing through her body. Gentle, then firm, they played with her until she was panting and squirming under his touch.

"Do you like that?"

"Oh God, yes."

"Then take your panties off for me, Chastity."

She reached down to pull them from her hips, when his hand covered hers, stopping the movement. She glanced at him, confused.

"Stand up and show me all of you again."

She bit her lip and moved away from him to reluctantly stand next to the bed. He placed a hand behind his head and watched her. The look in his eyes made her feel powerful and free. With a seductive smile, she hooked her thumbs into the sides and began to shove them over her hips and down her thighs. Shimmying, she flicked them to the floor and stepped out.

Dave sat up. "You're as stunning as I remember." He kissed her belly, then bent his head to the side and moved down to the top of her vulva in a long, sensuous lick. His hands stroked to her hips and he sank to the floor to kneel in front of her. The slightly abrasive tongue played over her vaginal lips, sending lightning flashes to her brain.

He pulled back and she pushed her hips forward. "I take it you want more?"

"Did I tell you that you're an ass?"

He chuckled. "Yep, at least twice."

"Good. Yes, I want more."

His answer was to part her nether lips with the finger of one hand and roughly tongue her clit. She gasped and almost dropped to the floor with the pleasure of it. His hand steadied her as he licked his tongue over and over the sensitive little button. She grasped his shoulders and let her arms support her upper body as she leaned her head back and enjoyed the thorough tonguing. Up and down, faster, then painfully slow and sensual. He seemed to know just when she was on the brink and altered his technique to better torture her. God, she wanted to come. She bucked her hips against his tongue, ran her fingers through his hair and placed his mouth hard against her clit.

With a grunt, Dave grabbed her wrists and pulled her hands to her sides, trapping them there.

The feel of this powerful man holding her back, holding her hands down was the most erotic thing she'd ever experienced.

Her legs shook and his tongue was replaced by teeth that gently nibbled her pussy lips.

"Oh God, Dave, please."

He chuckled and sucked her clit. Fast as lightning, he maneuvered both of her hands to one of his. With the free hand he reached up and moved over her buttocks. A finger played down her ass crack to the tender opening there. She struggled for breath and almost pulled away, but the assault on her pussy was too much. Running his fingers over her pussy, he caressed her asshole, moistening it. Lost in feeling, she was shocked when his fingers delved into her tight hole. She expected it to hurt, but any discomfort passed as he mouthed her clit and swiped a tongue over it. She screamed at the exotic mix of pleasure and pain and came, all but collapsing on the floor in front of him.

Bent over his body, she quaked with her orgasm. After a moment, he lifted her once more to the bed and laid her gently over the covers. Her eyes shot open as he ran a hand over her cheek, then pulled the boxers over his hips.

His cock bobbed out, long, thick and proud.

"You know, that monster is big enough for a porn flick."

He grinned. "I almost feel guilty being proud of it, since I had nothing to do with how it turned out."

She laughed. "Almost huh?"

"Yep." He reached into a bedside table and pulled out a box of condoms.

"Boy Scout?"

His brow knit in confusion. "Huh?"

"Be prepared." She tried to control the giggle, but it popped out anyway.

"My sister sends me these every year on my birthday. She thinks she's funny. I never took them on a trip, until..."

She blushed and looked away.

She heard the crinkle of the package and looked back. Dave stroked his cock a few times. "You ready for round two?"

"Ready, willing and able. I'm just worried about the fit. It was, um...a bit tight last time."

"I like it tight. Just the thought of you panting beneath me as I impale your pretty pink pussy makes me hard. Feel my cock, Chastity."

God she loved the way he talked when he was turned on.

He placed her hand over his cock and squeezed his fingers around hers while he stroked up and down its length. She licked her lips and he drew in a breath. "I don't think I can wait anymore. I want to fuck you."

She nodded and guided him towards her pussy. His breath quickened and he placed the tip against her entrance. "Slow and seductive, or hard and passionate?"

"Hmm, a choice. Well on one hand you have the seductive approach and on the other—"

He leaned in and growled in her ear. "You asked for it, lady." Grabbing her wrists, he forced them over her head. For a moment, she was stunned, then the feeling of being Dave Wellington's prisoner sent a shiver of need through her body.

Held down, he impaled her with his thick cock. The shock of it brought a cry to her lips, but the feeling of unbelievable fullness and his body pressed right against her clit were almost too pleasurable. God, how could she forget how good having sex with this man was?

He didn't give her a moment to get used to the fullness. Instead, he pulled all the way out and plunged back into her once more.

Pressure built within her as he fucked her hard, driving his thick penis into her willing cunt, over and over.

Just when she thought he would explode into her, he pulled his cock out. Confused, she blinked up at him. The look of devilment on his face sounded a warning bell in her mind a second too late. Roughly, he rolled her onto her stomach, pulling her ass in the air.

"Trust me?"

The need in his voice turned her on more than any of his actions. Did she trust him? She gave the barest of nods. His answer was the opening of the drawer on the night table.

Rolling over, she was rewarded with a sharp smack on her ass. The feeling was unlike anything she'd experienced before. Drawing in a gasp of pleasure, she stuck her bottom a little higher in the air.

He correctly interpreted her signal, because his hand connected with her bare skin once more.

"Do you like that, Chastity? Do you want me to spank your naughty ass, or tie you up and fuck it?"

The words rained down on her and turned her brain to fuzz.

"Tell me, Chastity, tell me what you want me to do to you." The bed creaked, and a hand touched her chin, urging her to look into his eyes. "Is this what you want? We don't have to. It's up to you. I'm happy with just fucking you."

"No, I like it. I like what you're doing to me. Please."

He smiled. The impish grin held something that made her heart race, but she didn't want to evaluate it now.

"Good."

He pulled her over his lap. The hand, when it connected with her already tender flesh, felt like fire rained down on her. One, two, three smacks across her bottom. Then, his fingers ran down between her ass cheeks, parting them. Something cool touched her tight hole, then a finger pressed against the opening. She clenched her cheeks, and another stinging swat was delivered.

"Relax. I won't hurt you. I promise."

"No, I'm nervous. I know you won't hurt me, but the pain..." She blushed.

"What, honey?"

"It feels sort of good. Does that make me a pervert?"

He chuckled. "Yes, but I like perverts. I want to hold you down and feel you squirm as I fuck your ass, Chastity."

"Yes. Please, yes."

She found herself on her knees, bottom in the air, as more of the lube was spread over her. The feeling of his cock pressed at the opening felt dirty, sexy and amazing. He pressed into her and she shook, almost pulling away. Hands grasped her hips, holding her in place as he inserted first an inch, then more. Soon she was stretched all the way out, filled with his huge cock.

What surprised her most was how good it felt. Incredibly good.

"Touch your clit while I fuck you. Make yourself come."

He didn't have to tell her twice. She adjusted herself so she could rub the hard button, gasping in pleasure at the feel of flesh on flesh.

"Oh God, Chastity, I'm going to come inside you, sweetheart." She moaned in answer and pushed her ass to meet him, thrust for thrust.

He pumped her hard and groaned as the waves of her own orgasm built over her. Wash after wash of pleasure moved through her brain as the cock in her tight ass pulsed with the unleashing of his orgasm.

She closed her eyes for a moment and felt his body, heavy and delicious, cover hers with a sigh.

Chapter Seven

Dave sat up, yawned and blinked. *What time is it?* His gaze lit on the clock in the corner. Seven thirty-six.

Something was off. He looked around. The lights weren't on, but a glow came from under the bedroom door. He furrowed his brow trying to remember. He swung his legs over the edge of the bed and memory flooded his brain. The beautiful, naked woman in his bed, the sex, the smell of her hair, the feel of her, warm and sweet against him. All of it. "Damn." What the hell had he done?

Hesitantly, he wrapped his robe around his shoulders and walked into the living room. A movement at the sink caught his eye. She stood there, disheveled and clean looking, with damp tendrils of hair clinging to her face from what he suspected was a shower. She smiled.

"Hi, um, I made coffee." Her hands fluttered in the air. Why was she so nervous? He ran a hand over his face. The indentations where he drew his eyebrows together were a telling clue. He must look like a grumbly old bear to her.

She pulled a chipped mug from the open shelves above the sink and poured a cup of coffee. "Sugar or cream? I don't know that. How can I not know that? I always know that about the men I—"

"Fuck?"

She looked up, her storm grey eyes wide with shock and what looked like hurt. Shit, he was being an ass. "I'm sorry. Black's fine."

She brightened. "Do you want breakfast? I can whip something up..."

He shrugged. "I don't normally eat anything but cereal, but if you'd like..." He sat and sipped the coffee, then pulled the mug back and looked down at the contents with a frown.

"Is something wrong?"

He jumped. She'd managed to sneak up behind him and drop a hand on his shoulder. He was pretty sure the gesture was meant to be comforting, but something about it made him nervous.

"No, the coffee's fine. It's just that..."

She sat across from him, another one of his chipped, mismatched mugs held tightly between her hands. "This is a little awkward?"

His smile felt grim. "It's not a typical morning after the night before. That's all."

She laughed. The sound was high-pitched and tremulous. Part of him wanted to comfort her, make small talk, eat a hearty breakfast, then... *Take her back to bed and fuck her senseless. Wake up, eat and do it again every day until he died.* Part of him wanted to run screaming into the woods like his brother had. He hid his emotions in a scalding sip of the dark brew. Damn, the woman was adorable, funny, smart, got to him sexually like no other woman ever had and made a fabulous cup of coffee. Too bad this would go no further. He put his cup down.

"Chastity—"

"Chas. My friends call me Chas."

He raised a brow. "And you've labeled me a friend?"

Her hands fluttered again, this time knocking over her almost empty coffee cup, spilling thick, dark liquid in a puddle over the polished maple of the table. She jumped to her feet. "Oh God, Dave. I am so sorry."

"It's all right. Just sit down. I'll get it."

He watched her place her hands on both cheeks for a moment, then drop them to her seat and clasp them together in her lap. Hair still damp, in a T-shirt and jeans, she looked young, vulnerable and totally adorable. He felt his cock twitch in appreciation. He frowned down at the table and began to wipe up the spilled coffee with sweeping strokes of paper towel.

"I'm sorry. I just don't know what to say right now. I mean. Well, I have stuff to say, but I don't know you, anything about you, not really and..."

He looked into her eyes. Tears gathered in the corners. A small movement drew his attention to her mouth, which trembled slightly. Oh crap, was he about to break her heart? No, she'd not known him long enough to have any real feelings and even if she did, she'd get over it. There was no room for a woman in his life. Especially a soft, vulnerable, smart and adorable woman he could... What? Fall in love with? Not likely. He fought back a snort of derision and sank back into his seat. No longer hot, the lukewarm sip tasted bitter on his tongue.

He leaned forward. "Look, what happened last night and back in March. Well, it wasn't a mistake, but... I'm not a man who sticks around long."

She stood, picked up her coffee cup and grabbed his out of his hand. With a toss of her head, she marched to the sink and began to hurriedly wash them.

"Chastity, I didn't mean to hurt you."

She turned then. Uh-oh, he'd made a mistake. She didn't look sad, she looked pissed. She took a deep breath and let it out slowly. "I see. You didn't mean to hurt me, just fuck me and move me on my merry way. Well then, all's fair. After all, it's what I did to you. I'll just gather my things and go. I can stay with my assistant tonight. She's supposed to have a private room, it's in her contract, but she'll get over it." She carefully dried her hands on the worn towel next to the sink and headed towards his bedroom.

He stood. "Chastity. Listen, it's not what you think."

He watched her stop mid-step and turn towards him. Her eyes narrowed and her hair slapped damply around her head.

"It's not? What I think is that you had some amazing sex with someone you never expected to have feelings for. I think that you're scared to death and are so used to your heart being a frozen barren wasteland that you're afraid you're going to melt if it's thawed." She took a step towards him and punctuated the words with points of her fingers. "I *think* that you are afraid you're going to end up just like your brother. Living alone on some homestead muttering to yourself about how unfair life is. That's what I think. Am I wrong?" She crossed her arms in front of her, clammed up and waited. Probably for a reply. His hand strayed to his hair and he pulled his fingers through it.

Now what? Tell her the truth? That she was closer than she knew? "Look, I know I'm an ass. I'm sorry, but what do you want from me? Marriage? Children? I'm not that guy. I'm a guy who—"

"Has one-night stands with women to prove he's a real man, then boots them out the next day when reality sets in?" She held up a hand. "Never mind, don't answer that. I don't really want to know the truth." Her hand swiped at her eyes. Shit, she was crying.

"I'm sorry, Chastity, I didn't mean to hurt you. I didn't plan any of this."

She pinched the skin at the bridge of her nose, nodded and sighed. "I know, Dave. I'm sorry. I'm equally responsible for last night. Especially after Chicago. I'd like to blame you, I really would, but I can't. I have terrible taste in men. You're just one in a long line of failures." She laughed. It sounded sad and off-kilter. "Oh well, at least my work here is a success. I have some women with some real prospects and you know what they say, those who can't do, teach." She hiccupped once, turned and disappeared into his bedroom. He thought about following her, but what for? What would he say? He was a heel. The dirty boot heel of the barn-mucking boots his dad used to wear. He sat back down at the table and hung his head in what he could only refer to as an old-fashioned sulk.

She wasn't long. In what seemed like only minutes she emerged from the bedroom, bags in hand. "I'm sorry to ask this, but..."

"Yep, I'll drive you into town."

She shook her head. "No, just my things. I think a walk will do me good. You can drop them off at the hotel."

"Are you sure?"

She nodded. "I think I need some space right now. I have some serious thinking to do."

Dave felt like an ass, but she was so close he drew her into his arms and placed his lips on hers. The kiss seemed to melt some of his pain, entwining them in a way he could not put into words. She pulled back first and looked up at him, the sorrow in her eyes spilling over in the form of silent tears. His heart lurched and he wiped the liquid that ran down her cheek with his thumb.

"Please, don't. I can't..."

"'The fault, dear Brutus, is not in our stars, but in ourselves, that we are underlings.'"

She smiled a half smile at him, reached up and caressed his face. "Julius Caesar." She turned and walked out of his life.

Chapter Eight

"You have got to snap out of it, girl. It's been a month already. Your mope time for boot man is so over."

She sighed. "You're right, Freddie. It's just that I got a letter from Poppy saying she's engaged to Bill and moving, lock, stock and barrel, to Smithfield, Alaska."

"Well I, for one, don't know why you're so surprised. There's someone for everyone. Even that horrible shrew."

Chastity sipped her orange spiced tea and made herself more comfortable. In the time she'd been home she'd spent a lot of her free time hiding out at Freddie's, hating her sterile apartment more and more. She loved her work and was busy scouting towns for next year, but her heart felt lost. She missed Dave. How the hell you could miss someone so much you knew so little was beyond her, but she did.

A finger snapped in front of her face. "You're not listening. Climb off the love train for a minute and pay attention to the bitchy diva."

"Oh for crying out loud, Freddie. I am most certainly *not* in love."

"You're floating down a river named denial and your barge is leaking there, Miss Cleopatra. Grab the asp already and deal with the poison. You're in love. Deeply in love, head over heels in love and he's a bazillion miles away. Sheesh, and you think I'm overdramatic."

Chastity's eyes went wide. "Oh dang."

"Oh dang, what?"

"Freddie, I'm in love with Dave like-the-boot Wellington."

"Well praise the Gods and pass the champagne. Now, what the hell are you going to do about it?"

She shrugged. "Nothing. He's out of my life. I just have to go on."

"Well damn, girl, fight for your man."

"I can't, Freddie. I feel like a big enough fool as it is."

"Well, if you're not willing to stalk the man to the point of a restraining order, can it really be love?"

She shook her head. "It was just one of those summer things." Damn, she was about to cry again. She'd been mopey as hell since she'd been home. Eating too much, then too little and sleeping more than she should. Crying was the last straw.

"Okay, which fabulous frock?"

She sat up. The least she could do was help Freddie put his ensemble together. It felt better when she got her mind off her own quagmire. "Hmmm, is the new boy-toy going to be there?"

Freddie nodded proudly.

"Then I think the silver lamé. It's over the top, but who else but a diva drag queen could carry it off?"

"God, you're fabu. How do you do it? Can I borrow your silver chandelier earrings?"

Chastity waved. "You can have them. I have no place to wear them. I'm reformed. I'll be a jeans and tight T-shirts girl from now on."

"Well, hallelujah, someone's starting to come around. Feel better since you admitted you love him, don't you?"

Chastity thought for a moment. "You know what? I think I do. Huh, imagine that. I almost feel normal, except for this big empty space."

"In your vagina?"

"*Freddie!* Shut up. I'm going to get the earrings now."

"Don't bother, honey. Sit there and ruminate on your lost love. I'll run and get them. You left it unlocked?"

Chastity nodded.

"Be right back then." He blew an air kiss her way and headed out the door.

Chastity smiled. Freddie had a way of picking her up when it seemed like the whole world was out to get her. She sipped her tea absently. She missed Dave, wanted to be with him. How the hell she managed to fall in love so damn fast was beyond her, but she did. Now that she acknowledged it, she knew in her gut she'd developed feelings and a connection for him that she'd not felt before. She hurt, but she'd get over it. It might take time, but she'd go on with her life. She was already busy planning next summer's assault on the Land of the Midnight Sun. Only this time, she was putting a chastity belt on first. She snorted.

"I crack myself up."

The door clicked open. "Find them, Freddie?"

"The course of true love never did run smooth."

Her head whipped around and she jumped to her feet, spilling the remains of her tea on Freddie's coffee table. "Oh my God..."

"You're supposed to say, 'A Midsummer Night's Dream'."

"I, uh, what are you doing here?"

"Looking for you. I ran into your neighbor. He said he needed some new nail polish and would be back in a bit. Nice guy." Dave took a step towards her. "Your friend—Freddie, was it?—mentioned you'd just had some epiphany regarding some guy from Alaska. Care to share?"

She blushed. "I, um, we were talking about you and he asked me a question. I said that I love you. What are you doing here?" She sucked in a breath to make up for the long one she'd let those words out on.

One more step brought him in front of her. "You love me?"

"Well, that's the gist of it. I want you to know you don't have to worry, I can get over you."

"I'm surprised."

She crossed her arms. "Why? Do you think you're so damn appealing that no one can get over you? Well, if you are—"

His hand came up and covered her mouth. "Chastity, I have something to say to you, but you won't hear it if you're busy berating me. Are you listening?"

She nodded.

"Good. What I meant to say is that I'm surprised you can get over me, 'cause I can't seem to get over you."

Eyes wide, she searched his face, but only saw sincerity and what looked suspiciously like love there. He let go of her mouth. "I've been waiting to do this for a month now." He pulled her close, placed his lips on hers and kissed her. His mouth felt so good and that smell that was all him wrapped around her like a warm blanket on a blustery night. He broke the kiss and pulled back.

"I love you and I was wondering if you'd like to try running your operation from Smithfield for a while to see how it goes between us. I wouldn't plan on moving back here though. I'd ask you to marry me tonight, if I didn't think I would scare you off."

"I thought you didn't believe in love and most especially, love at first sight?"

"Yeah, well as it turns out, I'm a moron."

She smiled and hugged him tight. "Yeah. I guess you are."

"Some Cupid kills with arrows, some with traps."

"'Much Ado About Nothing'?"

"Tricked into love. There's a moral there."

"That you're an overconfident ass, like Benedict?"

"Only without you."

About the Author

Nancy Liedel, writing as Nancy Lindquist, is the happily married mother of four boys (no, she is not going to try for a girl!). Two adopted and two made the old-fashioned way.

As a writer of erotic romance, Nancy is always taking mental notes wherever she goes. Nancy loves life and attacks it with gusto, leaving her wonderful husband and number one inspiration, Gene, to follow along laughing and shaking his head in her wake.

A lover of romance since she was passed *Shanna* under the table in tenth grade study hall by a friend of hers, Nancy finds the uninhibited world of Erotic Romance to be the perfect foil for her wit and naughty imagination.

To learn more about Nancy, please visit www.nancylindquist.com or visit her blog at www.blog.liedel.org. Send an email to Nancy at nancy@liedel.org.

Look for these titles by
Nancy Lindquist

Now Available:

How to Conjure a Man
Lady Lillian's Guide to Amazing Sex

Skin to Skin

Dionne Galace

Dedication

For Tim. My best friend, my partner in crime, the voice in my head. For Syd, who put up with my whining even as she cracked the whip. For Ann Aguirre, for being a good friend and my shining star.

Chapter One

"Fuck this heat!"

Leilani Howard stretched lazily on her lounger and glanced at the blonde perched on the wooden railing of her front porch wearing only a red bikini top and a pair of denim Daisy Dukes. "I told you we should have gone to the beach."

"Fuck the beach. You know it's going to be littered with noisy children greasy with sunblock lotion and their fat, hairy daddies ogling girls in bikinis." Jenna Harris plucked an ice cube from her glass of iced tea, sucked the sweet out of it and dropped it in her shorts. "Ahh...that's better."

"That's disgusting, Jenna. You're gonna get some sort of infection doing that." Leilani lay back against her lounger and rolled her own glass of iced tea across her forehead. "Besides, you're only contributing to the greenhouse effect with your yapping. If you just sit there and shut up, maybe you won't be so hot."

"God, you sound like my mother." Jenna unrolled her waist-length hair out of its topknot, shook it like a dog and rolled it back on top of her head. "Maybe you can ask your new neighbor if we can take a dip in his pool."

Leilani thought of the tall, muscular golden god who'd moved in next door just last month and felt her skin get hotter. *Oliver Clayton. God, even his name is hot.* She had been tossing and turning on her bed all week and it wasn't just because of the weather. The very thought of the man's big hands all over her skin had her pussy weeping and her body sweating all over the place. Too bad he was a first-class jerk. "I'd rather bake in my own sweat, thanks."

"Well, that's what's going to happen if we don't cool off right now." Jenna hopped off the railing and dropped her long, slender frame on the lounger next to Leilani. "Are you sure your AC is broken?"

"For the hundredth time, yes. And the repair company said they won't be able to get anyone out here till Tuesday." She lifted her black curls off her back and neck and secured them on top of her head with the scrunchie wrapped around her wrist. "Doesn't your apartment complex have a pool?"

"Oh please. With all the crackheads and hoodrats living in that place, I'd rather jump into a pile of used needles, thanks." Jenna picked up the Evian water spray and battery-operated mini-fan, pointed it at her face, turned it on and spritzed some water on the blades. "Man, that feels good." She turned the fan towards her friend and spritzed more water on the blades. "There. Feel the love."

Leilani lifted her face and welcomed the cool mist kissing her skin. "Ahh, you're a darling. If I paid you ten dollars an hour, would you do it for the rest of the day?"

"Hell, why not. I make about as much answering phones and being yelled at all day, anyway."

Leilani lowered her sunglasses and winked at her friend. "I'm totally joking about paying you, though. I'm as broke as you are."

"Bitch." Jenna switched off the fan and tossed it on the table next to the Evian spray and the pitcher of iced tea. "Are you sure we can't ask your neighbor about the pool? I'm dying here. All this heat is not good for my Nordic skin."

"Ugh. You ask him. Maybe he'll dig the tall Viking princess thing. He doesn't go for the lighter shade of brown, that's for sure," Leilani said with an affronted sniff.

"Wait, are you saying he shut you down? You, Miss Leilani I-Can-Get-Any-Man-I-Want Howard?" Jenna cackled and clapped her hands. "That's precious."

"Oh please, he didn't shut me down. He's probably racist. Or gay."

If there was one thing Leilani knew like the back of her hand, it was her effect on men. Courtesy of her African-American father, she had an all-year-long tan, a booty that wouldn't quit and curly black hair. The exotic tilt of her chocolate-brown eyes came from her *Sansei* mother. Men had been chasing her since she sprouted breasts in middle school. Because of her ass and tits, she looked older than she actually was and had men of all ages following her around. She wasn't supermodel-gorgeous—her nose was a little too big, and *lordy*, she loved to eat—but she had in spades what a lot of pretty girls didn't. Sex appeal. She knew how to move her body in a way that drove men crazy and didn't hesitate to use it to her advantage.

Which was why she didn't understand why Mr. Tall and Golden wasn't drooling over her. Last week, while he was washing his truck wearing cut-offs and nothing else, she passed by his front yard five or six times pretending to be walking her neighbor's dog Fifi, and he didn't look up once. She even put on her shortest skirt, a halter top that barely covered anything, and her super-special lip gloss that made Angelina Jolie's lips look anorexic. But no... He was so busy trying to make his stupid rims shine, he didn't even notice when she dropped Fifi's leash and bent over, flashing him her hot-pink thong.

"Wait, what do you mean racist? Are you telling me you've gone and gotten yourself smitten with a white man?"

Leilani looked up from slathering her leg with sunblock and threw a glare at her friend over her shoulder. "Who said anything about smitten? You're talking crazy."

Jenna rolled her big blue eyes. "Because we barely started talking about the dude and already you're getting ornery." The look on Leilani's face had her laughing and practically falling off her lounger. "You're totally sweet on him. Is he cute?"

Leilani waved her hand dismissively as though the very thought of the man didn't make her want to pour the entire pitcher of iced tea on her head. "Oh, he's all right. He's about six-three, tanned in a surfer boy way, green eyes...short blond hair"—*tousled like he just rolled out of bed and rubbed some gel on it*—"linebacker shoulders, eight-pack abs... Sure, he's cute. If you like that sort of thing." God, did she get breathless just talking about him? Damn that man.

"Mmm...sounds just like my type," Jenna replied, wiggling her blonde eyebrows suggestively. "Maybe I *should* go over there and ask if we could use his pool. Orrr...you could swim in his pool while he and I go swimming in his bathtub. And by swimming, I mean—"

"Jesus Christ, I get it!" Leilani slammed her glass on the table. Surprised at her own vehemence, she looked at Jenna, who was watching her with a Cheshire cat smile on her face. Embarrassed by her reaction to her friend's teasing, Leilani casually picked up the mini-fan, turned it on and aimed it at her overheated face. "Go on, then. Ask him."

Jenna smirked. "Not if you're going to break a glass and cut my throat with it."

"Shut up and go, Jenna. Jeez."

Jenna rose languidly from her lounger, shook her skinny butt at Leilani and strolled off of her front porch, fluttering her fingers in goodbye over her shoulder.

Leilani glared at her friend's back and folded her arms over her chest, pushing up her bikini-clad breasts. She wasn't going to watch. She wasn't. *Ugh!* Pushing her butt off the nylon lounger, she braced her arms on the wooden railing and followed Jenna's trek across her neighbor's yard with narrowed eyes. The woman had the gall to hop and skip like a bunny rabbit.

She swore to herself that if her neighbor ended up going for Jenna, she wasn't going to tear her hair out. She wasn't like that. Jenna had been her best friend since high school and no guy was ever going to get in between them. Still, the image of Jenna's long white limbs wrapped around the Adonis-like body of her neighbor had her blood boiling. Oh, hell, no... *I saw him first.*

Meanwhile, Jenna had already made it to her neighbor's front porch. Shaking her hair out of its topknot and propping her hand on one hip, she pressed the doorbell. As she waited for her quarry to answer the door, she turned her head towards Leilani and blew her a lascivious kiss. Leilani responded by flipping her middle finger at her.

After what seemed like an eternity, the front door opened and the hottie popped out wearing nothing but low-rise khaki shorts. A bead of sweat trickled from Leilani's forehead down to her breasts as she watched the two of them talking. Jenna did her thing, flipping her hair around and shaking her C-cups in a way that would have made Tawny Kitaen proud. Leilani groaned. *That's it. He's done for.* No mortal man had ever been able to resist Jenna's patented shake and jiggle. Leilani held her breath.

But the golden god looked more put-upon than anything. A grin slowly crawled across Leilani's full lips as Jenna's face darkened with outrage. She couldn't hear what they were saying, but Jenna looked like she was about to spit nails. Jenna started stabbing at Oliver's bare chest with her inch-long French tip, but the man merely shrugged in a Gallic way and shut the door in her face. Jenna whirled towards Leilani's porch, her face an unattractive red, and flung her hands in the air as if to say "I give up". Leilani struggled to keep herself from laughing, but managed it and summoned her friend back to her porch. Jenna made a screeching little noise that Leilani could hear even from her house and kicked the door.

Leilani couldn't help the laughter that burst out of her mouth as she watched Jenna limping across the yard. She laughed so hard that she was actually hiccupping by the time Jenna made it back to her porch. The blonde stomped up the steps and threw her a death glare that should have been scary, but only made her giggle again.

"Oh God," Leilani gasped, wiping at her eyes. "That was charming. You should have seen your face when he slammed the door on you."

"Shut up." Jenna dropped her weight on the lounger, removed her thong sandals and began to massage her big toe. "That man may be super hot, but you don't want him, sista. Trust me on this."

Leilani sat back down on her lounger, adjusting her frilly pink micro-skirt over her thighs. "Umm...is he gay?"

Jenna leveled a look on her. "God no. He's just... Oh, baby girl, he's a pig."

"Why, did he cast aspersions on your character and call you a triflin' ho?"

Jenna angrily combed her fingers through her hair, twisted it and piled it on top of her head. "No, dummy. He's a cop." She shuddered melodramatically. "Ugh, I can't believe I wasted my shake and jiggle on him. I feel dirty now."

"How could you tell he's a cop? Did he flash his badge at you?"

"Oh come on. The haircut, the way he talked, the way he stood... Eww, he even smelled like gun oil and Ivory soap." Jenna rubbed at her skin as though trying to get rid of dirt that Leilani couldn't see. "You can have him, girl. He prefers you anyway."

A cop. Huh. *No wonder he is such a hard ass.* Trying not to look too interested, she tucked a lock of hair behind her ear, adjusted her skirt again, and *then* she asked, "And how do you know that?"

"Girl, who are you fooling? You are totally hot for this man."

Leilani narrowed her eyes at her friend. "Don't play games with me. You *know* I can make you talk."

"All right, all right. Sheesh." Jenna smirked and picked up her iced tea, sipping slowly from the Krazy Straw Leilani had stuck in her glass. "So I go up there, knock on the door and ask Mr. Protect and Serve if you and I could take a dip in his pool. I tell him he could join us. I do my patented shake and jiggle. And he throws me this dirty look! I couldn't believe it. Anyway, he said no and closed the door."

Leilani gritted her teeth, but forced a smile on her lips. Jenna and her stupid games. When Jenna got the goods, it always took a little bit of arm-twisting to get her to talk. The girl could make a Buddhist monk scream. "And why does that mean he prefers me over you?"

Jenna rolled her eyes. "Because he said, and I quote, 'And you can tell your friend she can stop prancing in front of my house in her little outfits. I'm not buying,' end quote. Naturally that means he likes you."

Chapter Two

Oliver Clayton sipped his beer as he stared out of his living room window. It gave him a perfect view of his neighbor's front porch where she was now displaying her assets in a black bikini top and tiny pink thing that one could laughingly call a skirt. As he watched, she rose from her lounger, sauntered to the side of the house and turned on the sprinklers for her front yard. Laughing like little girls without a care in the world, she and her blonde friend danced and twirled around as the water drenched their tight bodies.

But he only had eyes for Leilani Howard. Christ, what a hottie. All that honey-colored skin, shiny black hair and such luscious pink lips that he got hard just thinking about them. And those eyes...those heart-stopping cat eyes that seemed to taunt him every time she looked at him.

He almost bumped into her yesterday as he was walking to the end of his driveway to pick up his newspaper and she was coming back from her morning jog. She was wearing a pair of black stretchy pants that clung to her heart-shaped ass and a hot pink sports bra that showed off her round, perky breasts. A bead of sweat trickled from the side of her face down to her neck then to the edge of her sports bra and his eyes had vigilantly tracked its movement. She was a little winded from her run, but the glow it brought to her cheeks and neck made her look more beautiful. Her Asiatic chocolate eyes seemed to taunt him, daring him to chase and catch her. For a brief moment, he actually considered taking her up on the invitation. Instead, he said nothing, saluted her with his newspaper and walked back to his house.

Outside, the blonde friend picked up a garden hose and sprayed Leilani in the face with it. Leilani shrieked and tried to get away from her friend. In the process, her long hair escaped its topknot, cascading down her shoulders and back like a black waterfall. Ollie groaned and rubbed his hardening cock through his shorts. If he'd only taken her up on her offer, he could be laying between her legs now, exploring her honeyed pussy with his tongue. Instead he was standing like a creepy old man by his window watching her and her friend go *Girls Gone Wild* on each other.

Now Leilani had control of the hose and was chasing her friend with it. The two of them fell to the grass, giggling and shrieking. For a brief moment, their faces were close enough together that Ollie was sure they were about to kiss. Had he read the signs wrong and Leilani was actually a lesbian? *No way. No woman looked at a man like that if she didn't want his cock deep inside her pussy. Right?* But what if he was wrong? Before he could start doubting himself, Leilani sprayed the friend in the face with a blast of water and the chase was on again. Damn, if he were a lesser man, he would be filming this shit and selling it on the Internet. *But that would be wrong.* Hell, all he wanted was to go out there and cover her with a giant towel so no one else could look at her.

Thankfully, a handful of neighborhood kids came over to join them dressed in bathing suits and carrying a colorful assortment of water toys. One of the mothers had brought over an inflatable pool that was less than three feet in diameter and Leilani helpfully filled it with water from the hose. The kids fought over who was going to get into the pool first, but Leilani mediated and had the kids settle it with Rock Paper Scissors.

As he watched the cheerful scene, Ollie felt like a selfish bastard. As far as he knew, he was the only one in the neighborhood with a pool. He could go out there and invite the kids as well as Leilani and her friend over for a swim. If it had been Leilani who'd asked him earlier, he wasn't sure he could have said no. But the thought of so many strangers invading his privacy made his skin crawl. And kids... Well, they were all right with him. In moderation. And in the presence of their parents.

Shutting the blinds on the window, Ollie limped over to the sofa and crashed, placing his injured leg on the ottoman. Grabbing his bottle of prescription Vicodin, he shook two tablets out to his palm, tossed them into his mouth and crunched them between his teeth, swallowing them dry. As he waited for the painkiller to take effect, he sank into the cushions of the couch and turned on the TV to the Discovery Channel, massaging his thigh.

It was a hell of a thing to take a vow of celibacy. But if a man got shot in the thigh over a woman with the bullet barely missing the important parts, he was allowed to reevaluate his priorities. Right now, getting involved with another woman was *not* one of his priorities. And that meant staying the hell away from Leilani Howard and her sexy cat eyes.

ॐ

Oliver woke up with a burning pain in his inner thigh. And a raging boner so hard and long it almost reached his navel.

God, that was a hell of a dream. Who knew a woman could even bend her body that way?

He reached for the bottle of Vicodin on the bedside table, threw a couple of tablets into his mouth and drowned them with a glass of water. Well, that would take care of the pain. He only wished it could kill his erection too. He grabbed the towel at the foot of his bed and wiped away the film of sweat on his bare shoulders. A sudden bolt of pain through his thigh had him hissing through his teeth and seeing stars in front of his eyes.

These dreams he'd been having about Leilani were going to kill him if the pain didn't beat her to it.

Yeah, he wasn't going to be able to sleep until the Vicodin kicked in and it was too damn hot to stay in his room. He picked up his boxers from the floor and slipped them on. After a moment, he decided to put on his jeans too, pressing down on his penis as he pulled the zipper over it. He thought about jacking off to relieve the pressure in his balls, but the pain in his thigh wasn't exactly sexually stimulating. He figured he'd sit on the patio with a beer until the pain subsided or he got sleepy. He could use the fresh air.

Popping open a can of beer, Oliver limped out to the patio, leaning against the railing for a moment so he could catch his breath. It was a little cooler outside than it was inside, but not by much. It did feel good to get out of the house, though. He was going fucking nuts in there. All he could think about was the pain in his damn leg or the sight of Leilani in her bikini rolling around in the grass. Neither was a particularly calming thought.

His cock throbbed like a living thing against his leg and he rubbed it absently through his jeans. The cold beer helped, but what he'd really like to do was go for a swim. That would definitely cool him off. Unfortunately, with his leg acting up, he would most likely drown and it would only be ironic justice for a guy who wouldn't let his neighbors swim in his pool.

There was the sound of a door opening and banging closed. Ollie raised his head in time to see Leilani walking out to her patio. He ducked behind a post and watched her stretch her slender arms over her head, thrusting her pert breasts forward. The movement caused her spaghetti-strapped tank top to pull up revealing a tanned, slightly rounded belly. For some reason, it turned Oliver on even more. He always liked a woman who wasn't afraid of food. The boxer shorts she was wearing were white sprinkled with red hearts and showed off her long, golden legs and plump ass. In the moonlight, with her wild black hair flowing freely around her shoulders, the woman resembled an Aztec goddess. Ollie's hand tightened around his beer can.

As though she sensed him looking at her, she turned towards his patio and squinted her eyes, her hands propped on her waist. Ollie pushed off from the post and braced his arms on the railing so she could see him better. Across the yard, she finally spotted him and waved hello. Against his better judgment, he waved back. She must have taken his greeting as an invitation because before he knew what was going on, she was crossing the yard in her bare feet and walking towards his house.

Damn the woman. She was going to be the death of him.

"Hello, Oliver," she said in that husky voice of hers, stepping up onto his porch. She nodded at the beer in his hand. "Got any more of those?"

Her neck and shoulders were glowing with sweat and gave her an otherworldly sheen. Oliver raked his gaze from the top of her hair down to her bare feet, then back up to the nipples poking through the thin material of her tank top. He could almost taste them in his mouth. He took a healthy gulp of his beer and swallowed hard. "Nope. Last one." He had a twelve-pack in the fridge, but that would mean limping into the kitchen and frankly, it was too far to limp and he was too goddamn tired.

She raised one perfectly tweezed eyebrow at him and smiled. "Do you mind if I have a sip?"

There was three feet of space between them. Ollie extended his arm, but didn't take a step towards her. If he got any closer, he was liable to grab her and pin her against the wall. "Here you go."

She sashayed towards him. He was entranced by the sight of her bellybutton. She was an innie. He felt like dropping on his knees in front of her and swirling his tongue into the tiny oval hole.

"Thank you." She accepted the can from him, licked the spot his lips had touched and tipped the can towards her open mouth. "Ahh, that's good."

She rolled the can over her chest and the condensation, along with the cool night air, made her nipples more visible through her shirt. Ollie groaned inwardly and massaged his thigh.

"Is something wrong?" she asked, looking down at his thigh. "Is it hurting you? I know a little massage. I can help you out, if you want." Her cat-like chocolate eyes blinked innocently.

Ollie realized his tongue had gotten stuck to the roof of his mouth and he couldn't say a word. The last thing he needed was this gorgeous woman kneeling between his legs attempting to massage his thigh when she should be massaging his cock. With her lips. He snatched the beer from her hands and poured the rest of it into his mouth. She looked up at him in surprise. "Sorry. Thirsty." He cleared his throat and rubbed the back of his neck. "What are you doing up, Leilani?"

She lifted her hair off her shoulders and the movement thrust her tits forward as though she were offering them to him. *Damned woman.* "Couldn't sleep. It's just too hot." She dropped her hair and her curls fell over her shoulders. She rolled her hips and took another step towards him, brushing her manicured nails against his bare chest. "And what are you doing *up,* Oliver?"

He felt himself grow harder at her blatant innuendo. She was so close he could smell her and he didn't know how much longer he could hold out. Her intoxicating scent was a combination of strawberries, cinnamon and hot summer night. God help him, but he wanted to know if she smelled like that everywhere. Before he could stop himself, he plucked one of her curls from her shoulder and used it to tug her closer. She braced her soft, cool hands against his chest and her lips quirked into a smile.

Lowering his head, he traced a line along the side of her neck with the tip of his tongue, which made her moan and press her crotch against the bulge in his jeans. He could take her now, if he wanted. He could brace her against the wall, lower her shorts, unzip his jeans and plunge his aching cock deep, deep inside her. He buried one hand in her hair and pulled her head back so he could continue his assault on her throat. She whimpered and began an agonizingly slow grind against his cock.

He groaned. But not from pleasure. A searing bolt of pain stabbed through his thigh and he almost passed out from the intensity of it. He quickly shoved her away from him, but grabbed her arm before she could fall flat on her ass.

"What the hell is wrong with you?" she demanded, pushing her hair out of her face.

"Sorry." The muscles in his upper thigh cramped up like a vise grip and he crushed the beer can in his fist, dropping it to the ground. Christ, it felt like molten lava had been poured into the old wound. Beads of sweat popped up on his upper lip and forehead and for a moment, he thought he was going to piss himself because of the pain. "Go home, Leilani. Get out of here."

"For God's sake, Oliver, what's going on?" She yanked her arm angrily from his grip, but remained maddeningly close to him. Placing her fingers under his chin, she lifted his head so she could look at his face. "Talk to me, are you in pain?" She pushed him aside for a moment, opened the door behind him and draped his arm around her shoulders. "Come on."

He attempted to pull away from her, but she held fast to him. "What are you going to do, carry me in? I'm two hundred and twenty-five pounds, lady. And what are you, one-ten, maybe one-fifteen?"

"Bless your heart, but no." She flashed a quick grin at him. "I do a bit of weightlifting at the gym, you know, and I come from sturdy stock." She slipped her arm around his waist and gave him a squeeze. "Now brace yourself on me, I'm gonna walk you in."

Ollie had his doubts, but somehow the two of them made it to the couch. He had always thought of her as a delicate orchid, pretty to look at, but ultimately useless and without much substance. He may have to reevaluate his opinion of her. She dropped him on the cushions, but somehow their legs got tangled together, and she ended up on top of him.

"Oh, isn't this interesting," she murmured, a small smile curling her full lips. She drew a circle around his cheekbone with a fingertip. "But I've never been one to take advantage of a sick man." She lifted her body off him and pulled him up so he was sitting upright. Brushing a lock of her hair out of her face, she gently picked up his injured leg and placed it on the ottoman. "Is there anything I can get you? Do you have anything for the pain?"

Ollie looked up at her face and saw something there that trapped the breath in his throat and had his heart pounding against his rib cage. She was more than beautiful in the moonlight shining through the window. She was...*ethereal*. And so immensely fuckable that his cock pleaded with him to just grab her. He had to get this woman out of his house now or he would never want to let her go. "I'm fine," he said hoarsely. "I've taken some Vicodin."

She raised an eyebrow and whistled through pursed lips. "An officer of the law taking narcotics. Heavy stuff." She took a throw pillow and squeezed it between his back and the couch cushions. Picking up his hand, she sat next to him and placed his palm on her bare thigh. "What's with the leg, anyway? Was it a gunshot wound?"

Ollie gritted his teeth. God, she smelled so good. He resisted the urge to stroke the soft flesh beneath his fingers. "Yeah."

She brushed her thumb over his temple. "How did it happen? Were you trying to be somebody's big hero?"

He grunted. "Something like that." And sticking his nose where it didn't belong.

"Wow, you're a talker, aren't you." She chuckled and grabbed the Kleenex box nearby. She pulled out a few sheets and leaned over him, dabbing at his forehead. "Look at you, you're sweating. Poor baby."

Her breasts hung over his face and one nipple was close enough he could have stuck out his tongue and licked it through the thin cotton covering it. He watched, mesmerized, as a bead of sweat trickled from the back of her ear, down her neck, disappearing into her cleavage. Saliva began to pool in his mouth. "I'm fine, Leilani. You can go now. The Vicodin is kicking in."

The corners of her lips quivered, but the teasing smile remained. "Are you sure you don't want me to give you a massage?" She waggled her fingers suggestively. "I'm really good with my hands."

Oh, I bet you are. "No," he said through gritted teeth. He shut his eyes for a moment. He didn't know how long he could keep himself from grabbing her around the waist, throwing her on the couch and taking what she clearly offered. He opened his eyes and forced a stern expression on his face. "Go home."

She stilled against him and rose gracefully from the couch. Pulling her tank top down so it covered her belly, she tilted her head to the side and a thoughtful look entered her eyes. "You're a hard man to know, Oliver Clayton."

"Maybe I'm just a man who prefers to be doing the chasing."

A corner of her mouth twitched and she gave him a brief nod. "Point taken." Without another word, she turned on her heel and walked out of his house. The door quietly clicked closed.

Ollie shoved his hands into his short blond hair and banged his head against the couch cushions. *That went well, Clayton. Asshole.* At least she wouldn't be bothering him anymore. She was driving him nuts with all those sexy outfits she'd been parading in front of him, showing off her honeyed skin. Though it killed him to think he would never see her in her stomach-baring, curve-hugging clothes again, he wished she would stay far, far away. It would be the best thing that could happen for the both of them.

As he sat in the dark contemplating his own stupidity, the pain in his thigh slowly subsided until it disappeared entirely.

Chapter Three

"Hope you're staying cool, San Diego, 'cause if you thought yesterday was a scorcher, today is gonna be a dooooooz..."

Leilani shut off the radio. She didn't need some hokey deejay telling her the Devil had come to town and brought the weather with him. She already knew she must have sweated at least ten pounds of water weight just this weekend alone.

She double-checked the fan pointed at her, but it was already set at full power. She stood up from her desk and removed her T-shirt, wiping the perspiration from her neck, breasts and armpits. Hell, she was hot enough that she was tempted to hack off her hair. She unbound it from its loosening topknot, re-twisted it and secured it with pins. She could take a shower again, but had already showered three times today, and frankly, a fourth time would just be...weird.

She switched off her computer and headed for the kitchen to get a can of pop. Throwing open the fridge door, she stood in the cold in her bra and panties and sighed with pleasure as the air glided over her skin. Maybe she could get her laptop, grab a chair and work inside the fridge all day. Mmm...that would be nice. And if she could somehow get Oliver Clayton to grovel at her feet, begging to suck her toes, life would be perfect.

At the thought of the man, Leilani's good mood evaporated. Taking a can of diet soda from the fridge and the pint of French vanilla ice cream she had in the freezer, she shut the door with her foot and brought the two items to the tiled island. God, just thinking of the man's name made her want to simultaneously scream and stick her head in a bucket of cold water. *Stupid, stubborn man.* Where did he get off playing hard to get with her? She had never had to chase a man in her entire life and couldn't believe he avoided her like she had leprosy when he was obviously interested. Hell, unless he sported a permanent erection in his pants, he wanted her as much as she wanted him.

She dropped two scoops of ice cream into a giant mug and poured the diet soda after it. She stuck a Krazy Straw into a floating mound of ice cream, grabbed a dessert spoon and strode towards the living room, flopping gracelessly on the couch. Turning on the TV, she flipped through several talk shows, a half a dozen soap operas, a couple of home improvement shows and finally settled on a Movie-of-The-Week starring Judith Light as an abusive housewife.

A few minutes into it, she looked down at herself and shook her head in disgust. "Look at me. I'm a good-looking sista and yet I'm sitting here in my drawers, watching a TV movie and stuffing my face with ice cream." She sighed and turned off the TV. "This is just sad."

Who the hell does Oliver Clayton think he is, anyway? But when she thought about him sitting in the dark, looking all defeated and telling her to go away in that agonized voice of his, something inside her just...broke. God, Jenna was right. She was smitten with the man and she didn't even know a damned thing about him.

Why did she have to fall for a guy like him? *Fall? Whoa, back up, Leilani. You don't even know the dude.* It was just a *Jungle Fever* thing, that's all, a novelty. And he was so very different from all the other guys she had dated in the past. She

163

didn't even like white guys. She liked them darker than chocolate and smoother than silk...a fine-ass brother like Denzel Washington. Or olive-skinned and whipcord-lean like Takeshi Kaneshiro. She didn't need some blond-haired, green-eyed surfer type treating her like gum stuck under his shoe and trampling all over her heart.

I'm fine, Leilani. You can go now. Ugh. She couldn't believe how dismissive he'd been of her. The man irritated her like no other had ever done. Sometimes, all she had to do was think his name and her blood— Oh, who was she kidding? She was one hundred percent, over-the-moon, batshit crazy over the guy.

Before last night, she had never even had a conversation with him. Sure, they may have said hello to each other in the past... Okay, she said hello and he grunted. Not that he really had to say *anything*. From the moment he turned those heartbreaking green eyes on her, she was lost. It sounded cheesy even to her, but every time he looked at her, she felt like throwing her arms around him and never letting go. For all she knew, the man could be a complete imbecile, but somehow that didn't seem possible. There was quiet intelligence in those mesmerizing eyes...an intensity that had her head spinning and her knees melting. She didn't even want to think about his effect on her panties.

She slammed her mug of Diet Coke float on the coffee table and sprang up from the couch. She had to get out of the house or she was going to go nuts mooning over Oliver frickin' Clayton. But where would she go? It was early in the afternoon, so if she went to the mall, she'd be bumping into secretary-types shopping on their lunch break or kids with nothing better to do but hang out at the food court. She didn't want to go to the beach because she had never been a fan of the sand, and salt water had a tendency to wreak havoc on her hair.

What was it about the man that made her feel like a teenager with a first crush when she was a grown woman a stone's throw away from thirty?

What would really make her feel better would be a cool dip. Preferably in somebody's pool. And she did not mean the YMCA. She propped her hands on her hips and bit her lower lip. Well, it was the middle of the day. What were the chances that Oliver would be home? Didn't cops usually work in the daytime?

She peeked her head out of the front door, but didn't see his white Dodge Ram pickup in front of his house. And there was no way he could fit that gigantic sucker inside the garage. What was it with men and big-ass cars? Normally, she would have thought he was overcompensating, but she had felt that steel-hard cock against her crotch. There was no way the dude was compensating for anything.

She could almost feel that cool, clean water closing over her head now, running over her skin like silk. Maybe all she needed to get that man out of her head was a nice, long swim. And she knew the pool was clean because she watched him just last week diligently cleaning it in his denim cut-offs. That is, she stood on a stepstool and peeked over the fence. She'd been slick about it too. He had no idea she had watched him until she got a cramp in her leg. God, she creeped herself out sometimes.

She hurriedly put on her swimsuit—white top and white bottom decorated with hot pink hibiscus flowers—and tied a hot pink sarong around her middle. Grabbing a towel and a bottle of sunblock, she made her way to the front porch and slipped her feet into her pink and white thong sandals. She looked up and down the street to make sure no one could see her, then crossed into Oliver's yard and crept towards the side of his house. Checking over her shoulder one last time, she pushed at the wooden gate to his backyard and frowned when it didn't budge. Well, hell, didn't anyone trust the inherent goodness in people anymore?

"Stupid paranoid cop." She glanced around her immediate area for a stick with which she could lift the latch. "A-ha!"

Within seconds she was in, closing the gate quietly behind her. The kidney-shaped pool was now just about ten feet away from her and looking at the cool blue water, she shivered in anticipation. God, she couldn't wait to jump in.

She approached it with the reverence of a child given a ten dollar bill at a candy store and instructed to go nuts. She stopped at the edge and dipped her big toe into the water, biting her lower lip to keep herself from moaning out loud. Oh, it was going to be *so good.* But first thing's first. Dropping her sarong on a lounger, she sat down so she could rub sunblock on her skin. While her hands glided smoothly over her breasts and inner thighs, she imagined they were Oliver's hands touching her, rolling and plucking at her nipples with those long, nimble fingers. Unfortunately, she only succeeded in creaming her bikini bottoms and making herself more sexually frustrated than she already was.

With a sigh, she took her hands away from her body and stood up from the lounger. Yes, she needed to wash that man outta her mind. "Better do some stretches first. Don't wanna get a cramp. No lifeguard on duty," she muttered.

Raising her right leg straight out behind her, she dropped forward and pressed her fingers on the white tile, curling her leg until it was almost touching her spine. She held the pose for a minute then slowly lowered the leg. Taking a deep breath, she did the same for her other leg and held the pose until she could feel a slight burn in her thigh. Afterwards, she stood up straight and did a few side twists with her hips, then a couple of toe touches.

And finally, she was ready. Oh, how she truly savored this moment. If only Jenna could see her now. She looked around Oliver's neat little yard with a sense of triumph. God, she was so slick sometimes, she scared herself.

With a grin on her face, she swung her arms over her head and dove into the cool blue water.

Chapter Four

It's all in my head. The stabbing pain in his old GSW...the cause of it was all in his head.

After waking this morning feeling as though little red ants were crawling inside his thigh—and incidentally, with an impossibly hard erection courtesy of an X-rated dream starring his beautiful neighbor—he finally gave in and called his doctor, an old buddy from college. He also phoned his captain to let him know he wasn't going to make it in and drove to his buddy's practice across town.

Bill Crenshaw poked and prodded the wound to check it for infection, but found nothing. He asked about Ollie's physical therapy as well as his daily care and treatment of the wound, complimented him on the rapid healing of it, and told him he should be able to return to active duty in no time.

"But Bill, the leg—" Shit, how was he going to explain this without sounding like a fool? Ollie rubbed the back of his neck in embarrassment. "Umm, how the hell do you explain the pain I get in there when I..."

Bill patted his shoulder encouragingly and put on his best trust-me face. "Go on, son, you can tell me. It won't leave this room, I swear."

Ollie looked up and narrowed his eyes at his friend. Not only was the bastard being overly solicitous, he called him "son". And he was only two months older than Ollie. "Aw, fuck you, Crenshaw. Get out of here with this shit."

His friend widened his eyes innocently. "Well, hell, Clayton, how am I supposed to help you out when you can't tell me what's wrong?"

"I swear to God, Bill, if you tell any of the guys about this, I'm going to dig deep into your past and find something—anything—that I can pin on you, so I can throw your ass in jail."

"I'm squeaky clean," Bill responded with a smirk.

Ollie flashed his teeth at him. "I'm a really good cop."

Bill raised his hands in mock surrender. "It's not like I can tell the newspapers, man. I'm sure you've heard of a little something called patient-doctor confidentiality."

Ollie ran his hand through his hair and exhaled heavily. "Umm...all right. Well, whenever I..." He cleared his throat. "Umm. Whenever I—"

Bill looked at him in exasperation. "Oh, for the love of Pete, Clayton, butch up and just spit it out."

"Fuck off, I'm getting there." Oliver rubbed his eyebrow and sighed. The best way to say it was quick and fast. Bill was a professional. He wouldn't fall down on his ass laughing. Probably. "The wound only really hurts when I get an erection." The words tumbled out of his mouth in a rush.

To his credit, Bill didn't burst into a guffaw. Instead, he looked gravely at Ollie and whistled through his teeth. "Well, hell. I've seen that neighbor of yours with the—" He held both of his palms in front of his chest. "The hot black chick with the booty that won't quit. Shit, man, it's a miracle you haven't come to me before now and begged for an amputation." He lifted his shoulders. "Short of an MRI to see if there's a clot in your thigh or something, I don't know what to tell you."

Every part of Ollie's body went still at that moment as he stared at his friend.

"Ollie, either it's all in your head or there's something physiologically wrong with you that I can't see. I suggest we go to the hospital right now and get you an MRI to find out."

A good friend cancels all of his morning appointments and goes with you to the hospital, just so he can be right there with you when the radiologist tells you there is nothing wrong with your leg. And then he laughs at you and tells you you're insane. Sitting in the hospital cafeteria, Ollie looked at his friend across the table and almost wished he hadn't saved him from getting his ass kicked by the frat dicks that day all those years ago.

"When did the pain start anyway?"

"About a month ago, two months after I got shot." Ollie sipped his coffee, grimaced, double-checked to see he wasn't actually drinking battery acid, then drank another mouthful. "The first time it happened, I thought I pulled my groin moving the furniture or something."

"Was that also the first time you saw the hot black chick with the tits?"

Ollie set down his cup of coffee and glared at Bill. "Her name is Leilani, all right?" He paused and narrowed his eyes. "Wait, what are you saying?"

Bill raised his eyebrows. "Jeez, Ollie. For a hotshot detective, you're pretty damn dense, you know that?" At his friend's blank look, Bill shook his head in disgust. "Before you got shot, you were feeling pretty lucky, right? Probably thinking you're gonna get to have sex with that gorgeous redhead. So up to the point the redhead's boyfriend burst into the room and shot you, you had an erection."

He met the woman in Vegas during a cop convention. He was nursing a scotch in the dark corner of the hotel bar when the gorgeous redhead sidled up next to him, rubbed her tits against his arm and invited him to her hotel room. He'd been feeling pretty lonely and was already more than a little drunk at the time, so he figured, why the hell not. He just didn't figure on being the unwitting pawn in the middle of a psychotic lovers' quarrel. "Like you wouldn't believe," he muttered.

"Well, the mind's a funny thing. Somehow, your brain now believes that an erection is very, very bad for you. To protect you, it sends a little message to your leg to remind you what happened the last time you got a little horny." With a smirk, Bill sat back in his chair and folded his arms across his chest, looking pretty pleased with himself. "And that, my friend, is why your GSW hurts whenever you have an erection. I can get you a psych consult, if you want."

Ollie didn't want to admit it, but the smug bastard had a point. His thigh only seemed to hurt whenever Leilani was around. "I don't need a shrink, thanks. I'm fine." He crushed the empty Styrofoam cup in his hand and sighed. "I'm probably never going to have sex again, but I'm fine." He remembered the feel of her silky skin under his tongue and sure enough, his thigh began to throb.

"Hey, it's all in your head, buddy. *You* need to take control now. If you really want this woman, you need to tell your brain what's up and go after her."

୫

It's all in your head, Clayton. Not that knowing that made any difference. All he had to do was think about how Leilani's breast would fit in his palm and his GSW shrieked in pain. Even now he could smell her clean cinnamon scent in his nose and see her sly, taunting smile when he closed his eyes.

Outside of a lobotomy, there was no getting away from the woman. Not when she'd gotten so deep underneath his skin.

Intellectually, he knew Leilani was worlds different from the crazy redhead he met at the bar. After all, the redhead turned out to be a chronic drug-user and a part-time hooker who had an arrest record as long as his arm. Leilani, however, graduated in the top of her class at UCSD with a degree in computer science, had a house of her own, and had never even received as much as a speeding ticket in her entire life. Of course, he could easily see himself pulling her over and letting her off with a warning when she flashed those mischievous eyes at him.

Obviously he'd had time to investigate her while playing desk jockey at the precinct.

In short, she was a classy lady who exuded grace and sensuality with her every move. And a damn sight better than a corn-fed Illinois boy like him deserved.

He shut off his truck and massaged his thigh. There had to be a way to resolve this once and for all. Every waking moment he'd had since he met the woman had been spent obsessing over her, imagining how it would feel to have her in his arms. Now that he knew, all he could think about was how to get her back there.

He pulled up his shirt and used the hem to wipe the sweat on his forehead. Maybe he could go for a dip in the pool. He wouldn't have to swim. He could just stay in the shallow end until the pain in his thigh subsided. With luck, his cock would also settle down in the water.

Taking care not to jostle his thigh, he carefully climbed out of his truck and limped towards his front door. As soon as he got inside the house, he removed his shirt and groaned as the AC cooled the film of sweat that covered his upper body. He braced his arm against the wall for a moment and stood under the vent, luxuriating in the cold air sweeping over his skin. After a few minutes, his erection went down and the pain in his thigh subsided, allowing him to walk to the kitchen without limping. He opened the fridge, grabbed a can of beer and popped it open, tipping the can towards his mouth. He finished the can in a few healthy gulps, crushed it in his fist and tossed it into the bin under the sink. Feeling reasonably refreshed, he headed for the sliding glass door that exited to his backyard and froze.

There was someone swimming in his pool.

"Well, I'll be damned."

With a grin slowly crawling across his lips, he turned on his heel and strode towards his home office. It was where he kept an extra pair of handcuffs.

As soon as Leilani surfaced from the pool, she immediately realized something was wrong. *Okay...no longer alone.* Her nipples stiffened in awareness and her skin tingled with the sensation of being watched. She folded her arms protectively across her breasts—oh, why the hell did she take off her bikini top?—and turned around.

Oliver Clayton was sitting on a lounger just a few feet away from her wearing only a pair of red board shorts, holding a pair of handcuffs and twirling her white bikini top around his index finger.

Leilani was entranced by the shiny metal twinkling in the sun even as she swallowed nervously and kicked backwards in the water to get away from him. A quiet menace radiated from the man. He reminded her of a panther, crouched and waiting for the perfect moment to spring. He was dangerous, a threat to both her body and her heart. In response to his nearness, her pussy wept silky cream in her bikini bottoms and she instinctively crossed her legs in futility to stave off the flow.

"I can arrest you for trespassing, you know," he murmured, his hunter-green eyes glinting with both threat and promise. "I might even have enough evidence to charge you with breaking and entering." He flashed his straight white teeth at her. "Now should we deal with it here or do I have to drag your pretty ass to the precinct?"

"You wouldn't." Even though the water wasn't cold, goose bumps sprouted all over her body. Her nipples became as stiff as pencil erasers and poked against the skin of her arm. "You can toss me my top and I can leave, Mr. Clayton. We don't have to make a big deal out of this."

"Mister?" He raised an eyebrow. "I prefer Detective Clayton, thank you. And you have to know I can't just let you go. What message would I be sending if I did that? That anyone can just break into my backyard and swim in my pool without my permission?" He shook his head. "No, I have to make an example out of you, Leilani."

Leilani shivered in spite of herself. Watching the man warily, she vigorously rubbed at her arms in an attempt to get rid of her goose bumps. What did she really know about the man? For all she knew, he had a hidden room in his house where he tied up his victims and sexually tortured them. "What are you going to do to me?" God, did she have to sound so breathless?

One corner of his mouth quirked and a dimple popped out in his cheek, matching the one on his chin. "You'll find out in due time." He jiggled the handcuffs in front of her. "Get out of the water, darlin'. Let's go. Nice and slow now."

Leilani gulped and took another step backwards. A few more steps and the water would be closing over her head.

Maybe she could swim quickly to the other side, climb out of the pool and run out of the backyard. Once she was in her house, she could lock all the doors and windows and pray he didn't come after her. But she didn't do any of that.

Instead she stayed where she was, shaking like a damned fool. She was sure he wouldn't hurt her, but she wasn't sure about the look glittering in his eyes. It bothered her how much it scared and excited her at the same time. She was tempted to tell him to come and get her if he wanted her, but her gaze drifted to his thigh. What if it cramped up again and he drowned? She wouldn't be able to pull that big, muscular body out of the pool. She didn't necessarily take pleasure in the crush she was nursing for the stubborn, grumpy bastard, but she didn't want him to die, either.

"Are you going to come out of the water or do I have to drag you out?"

A part of her thought she should be outraged that he would dare talk to her like this, but even that gave way to desire and hunger. For a whole month she had been going crazy wondering how his lips would feel on hers or how his mouth would feel on her breasts. Looking into his eyes, she realized there was something underneath the predatory gaze. *Vulnerability.* He was silently telling her to trust him.

Leilani suppressed the smile tugging at her lips. So her cop wanted to play, did he? Oh yes, she'd play. Taking a deep breath and hoping she wasn't going to regret it, she slowly lowered her arms and allowed him to look his fill.

Let the games begin, Detective.

Chapter Five

Leilani dropped her arms to her sides and Ollie almost fell out of his chair. The handcuffs slid out of his hands, landing on the grass. *So much for keeping my cool.*

Her breasts were just as he imagined them. Round, perky and tipped with dark brown nipples that looked like Hershey's Kisses. He couldn't wait to touch them, to suckle and nibble on those nipples. His mouth watered at the thought. His eyes followed the natural line of her body, her exposed belly, the tapered waist and the generous flare of her hips. Her bottom was covered by a white scrap of cloth that was barely holding on for dear life.

Reaching down, he felt around the grass for his handcuffs and was thankful when he found them quickly enough. He wrapped his fingers around the cool metal just as Leilani got to the edge of the pool and began to gracefully pull herself out on the rungs. He could have gotten up to help her, but at that moment, his thigh had begun to throb and frankly, the way his cock was threatening to poke a hole through his shorts told him standing up probably wouldn't be a good idea.

He surreptitiously snuck a hand down to his inner thigh to rub the area around his wound. It wasn't hurting yet, but the throbbing was definitely a warning. *Not now,* he prayed silently. *Please not now.*

Leilani stood before him, confident in her near-nudity, one arm hanging loosely by her side and the other propped on her hip. Her dark eyes belied her curiosity, but her lips were pursed in a sensual smile. Her curly mane was scraped back in a ponytail, serving to emphasize her long neck and the delicate bones in her face. Beads of water dotted her lips and neck as well as the valley between her breasts and he couldn't decide which part he wanted to lick first.

"Take down your hair," he ordered hoarsely.

Leilani raised one eyebrow, but reached up to pull off the scrunchie holding her ponytail, sending a cascade of black curls over her shoulders and back. One errant curl teased her nipple. With her hair loose, he decided she looked more like a Polynesian princess.

For a brief moment, he had a vision of himself lying in a hammock on a desert island somewhere sipping on a piña colada while Leilani danced in front of him in nothing but a grass skirt and her hair draped over her breasts.

"Will you give me back my top?" She nodded at the tiny piece of white fabric clenched in his fist. "Or are we going to do this naked?"

He looked down at the bikini top tangled with his fingers. "No, you're not going to get this back." Raising his head to look at her, he reared his arm back and flung the bikini top into the pool. "You don't need to be wearing anything for what I'm going to do to you."

"Well, I guess that means I have to take this off too." She hooked her thumbs into her bikini bottoms and did a little shimmy, but didn't take them off. As she studied him from beneath the veil of her lashes, the tip of her pink tongue peeked out and touched the corner of her lips. "What *are* you going to do to me, Detective?"

Staring at the expanse of brown flesh before him, at the enticing dip in her navel, and those long, slender legs that could easily wrap around his hips, a hint of insecurity began to nibble at him. What if his leg cramped up in the middle of their lovemaking and they had to stop? He jiggled the handcuffs uncertainly in his hand. He felt kind of stupid for bringing them out now. What the hell did he think he was actually going to do with them?

He looked up at Leilani's face and could see she was struggling to keep her flirtatious expression. She arranged her hair so it covered her breasts more adequately, and placed both hands on her hips for a moment before dropping them again so they hung at her sides. The teasing glint that was just in her chocolate eyes faded until she stood before him shifting uncomfortably from one foot to the other.

"Um...I should go." She jerked a thumb over her shoulder. "I'm just going to grab my stuff and get out of here. I'm sorry for trespassing."

Damn, he'd lost her. He resisted the urge to slam his palm into his forehead and call himself an idiot. He took a deep breath and slowly released it in an effort to regain his composure. "Your top is underwater in the middle of my pool. Are you seriously going to go home dressed only in those skimpy bottoms?"

A tiny knot appeared between her brows. "No, I brought my sarong with— Oh, fuck it, Oliver. You want nothing to do with me. I get it. I'll stop bothering you, okay?" She ran a hand over her hair, inadvertently flashing him her tits again, but realized what she was doing and blushed, crossing her arms securely over her chest. "I...I'm just gonna go while I still have some dignity left, thanks."

"Sit down, Leilani."

She raised her eyebrows in surprise, then shook her head. "No. I'm going home. You're probably not going to see me for a while. For the next few years, I'll be very busy trying to avoid you."

"I wasn't asking, Leilani."

"I..." Looking adorably flustered, she sat on the lounger next to him, her bare thigh only inches from his.

He stopped thinking. Stopped worrying. And for once just went with the flow. He cupped her face between his hands and brushed his lips against hers. She stilled against him, then placed her hands around his wrists to tug them away from her head.

"This isn't going to work, Oliver. I'm just gonna..."

"Shut up." He buried his hands in her silky-soft hair and used his grip on her to pull her close. "You're so fucking beautiful, you know that?" Without waiting for her response, he lowered his head and covered her mouth with his own.

He took his time tasting her, painting her lips with the tip of his tongue before plunging deep and devouring her. After what felt like an eternity, she responded, moaning into his mouth and sucking his tongue into her own. He nibbled on her lower lip, then the upper one, savoring the exotic taste of her. She tasted like vanilla and something he couldn't quite define. Whatever it was, it made his head swim and he couldn't get enough of it. He brushed his tongue over her teeth before sweeping into her mouth to taste her again.

She leaned into him, placing her palm on the lounger between his thighs for leverage and her other hand on his bare chest. She replaced her hand with her breasts, rubbing her nipples against him. Without taking her mouth away from his, she rose again, but only to put one leg over him so that she was straddling him and sat down again. Ever so slowly, she began to grind her crotch against his cock, stroking the length with her mound while she feasted on his mouth.

He could feel her heat through her bikini bottoms and the nylon of his board shorts and he wanted more of it. He felt like shoving down his shorts, pushing aside her bikini bottoms and just plunging into her. Hell, if she didn't stop gyrating against him like that, he wasn't going to last very long. His dick felt longer and harder than it had ever been before, and he felt no pain in his thigh except for the sporadic twinge of discomfort. It throbbed threateningly, probably gathering up all the pain receptors in his body, so they could all explode at the same time and kill him.

But at least he would die in Leilani's arms with the taste of her mouth on his tongue and her breasts pillowed against his chest.

But he had to slow things down now. His hands untangled themselves from her hair and swept down her neck, past her shoulders, brushing along the length of her arms until they reached her wrists. He pulled his mouth from hers with a pop and she mewled in protest. "Shhh, baby. We're far from done, don't worry." He lowered his head and sucked one brown nipple between his teeth. She resumed moaning in pleasure.

While she was distracted, he gently tugged her hands to her sides, stroking the skin below her elbow. He maneuvered her wrists so they were resting along her spine and encircled the both of them with one hand. When he had them in position, he raised his head from her breasts and looked at her flushed face. Her swollen lips parted in a small, shy smile.

He almost felt guilty for what he was about to do to her. Almost.

"Hello," she murmured, brushing her nose against his.

"Hello." He smiled back and clapped the handcuffs around her wrists.

Leilani's passion-hazed eyes widened at the distinct *click* of the handcuffs. Her mouth opened and closed as though she wanted to say a lot of things, but couldn't quite decide which one to say first. She shrugged off his hand as she flexed her arms, testing the security of her restraints.

"Omigod." The handcuffs clinked behind her as she wiggled her arms. She made a squealing sound of frustration when they didn't budge. Her lips pursed in annoyance as she narrowed her eyes at him. "Damn it, Oliver, I didn't think you were actually going to use these stupid things. Let me go now."

With her hands bound against her back, her breasts thrust forward, bobbing under his chin as she continued to struggle. Ollie groaned inwardly, but managed to keep the stern expression on his face. "No, baby, I'm not going to let you go. You deserve a little payback for the entire month you've been teasing me, shaking that sexy ass at me in your hot little outfits." He dug one hand into her dark mane and yanked her head back. "I'm going to kiss you all over, nibble on you, until every single part of your body has been touched by my mouth." He bent his head and sucked the skin under her chin between his teeth, laving it with his tongue. "And when you're quivering under me, screaming my name and begging me to take you, I'm going to fuck you so hard, you won't walk right for a week."

Leilani moaned and ground her crotch against his cock. "Oh, Ollie, we don't have to go through all that. I'm pretty easy. We can do it right now, if you want."

"No, no, baby. We're gonna do this my way." Ollie dragged his open mouth from her neck to her collarbone, tracing her sternum with the tip of his tongue. When he reached her breasts, he slid his hand from her hip to the underside of one breast and flicked the chocolate-colored nipple with his thumb. "I'm gonna make you scream my name so much you're gonna forget your own."

Ollie couldn't control the shaking he felt in his hand as he continued to explore her breasts. Her skin was so soft and smelled so good that he could barely restrain himself from tearing off her bottoms and thrusting his cock deep into her pussy. He circled her areola with his tongue and watched as her eyes drifted shut in pleasure, biting her lower lip as though she were keeping herself from crying out loud.

With his index finger, he drew a path from her rib cage down to her navel, dipping briefly into it, before continuing his descent to the garter of her bikini bottoms.

He could smell her need for him, that sharp musk of feminine arousal that signaled her excitement. When his fingers encountered the damp crotch of her bottoms, he pinched her clit gently through the material and was rewarded with a hot gush of cream. He pushed aside the white cloth and whistled softly when he discovered there wasn't a trace of hair on her pussy. With the tip of his finger, he traced a line along the slick folds and sank knuckle-deep into her, groaning when her moist, silky warmth closed around him. Raising his eyes to meet hers, he drew his finger out of her and brought it to his mouth, sucking at the dewy moisture. She looked longingly at his lips and licked her own in response.

He was right. She did taste like honey, a veritable ambrosia. He couldn't wait to feast on her. He couldn't wait to plunge his tongue into her pussy and suck out her cream. But he couldn't very well do that in his backyard where any perv with binoculars could be watching them. And he needed her to be comfortable for what he had planned.

"Ollie, please..."

"Damn, you're on fire," he murmured, pulling her face to his and allowing her to lick his lips so she could taste herself on him. "Why don't we take this inside." Without waiting for her response, he swept her easily into his arms and rose from the lounger, holding her tight against his chest. "I'd ask you to hold on to me, but you can't exactly do that, can you?" He smirked. "Don't worry, Leilani. I won't drop you."

Leilani squeaked and pressed herself against him. "Ollie, your leg!"

"It's all right. Now hush and let me take care of you." Oddly enough, he had completely forgotten about his wound until she mentioned it. It throbbed if only to remind him it was there, but otherwise it didn't really bother him. And his dick was hard enough to smash bricks.

He took her into the house and set her on the edge of his dining table. She looked up curiously at him and bit her lower lip, but didn't say anything. It was enough that those sexy cat eyes of hers penetrated through his soul. He placed his hand against her warm cheek and she turned her face towards it, pressing her lips to the center of his palm. At that moment, it hit him how beautiful she truly was and he had to grip the corner of the table to keep himself from falling down to his knees to worship her. "Lay down on the table, sweetheart," he ordered thickly.

Her lips quirked at the corners in response, but she remained silent. With a breathy sigh, she lowered herself onto the shiny mahogany even as her legs dangled over the edge. She managed to look graceful even though her arms were still awkwardly bound behind her.

For a moment, Ollie was entranced by the sight of Leilani lying on the dinner table, her breasts bare for his eyes and mouth to devour and her silky hair spread across the dark wood. He could have stared at her forever, but it was obvious from the strain on her face that she wasn't entirely comfortable laying on her arms. *Good one, Ollie. Way to be smooth.* He was about to reach into his pocket for the keys to free her when she lifted her head from the table and smiled at him.

"This is just a suggestion," she said, "but if you have another pair of cuffs, you could bind each of my wrists separately to the legs of the table."

He raised his eyebrows. Well, *damn.* Here's a woman who knew what she wanted and how to ask for it. God, he was going to have so much fun with her. He lowered his head and pressed a kiss on her abdomen. "I'll be right back. Stay here."

She flashed him a saucy smile. "Oh, I'm not going anywhere, baby."

He ran to his office, grabbed his other pair of handcuffs from the desk drawer and dashed back to her side. He reached into his pocket for the keys and gently rolled her to her side so he could unlock one cuff. "Scoot over to the other side of the table."

She did as he asked, bending over to crawl across the table. Ollie couldn't help but grab a handful of her plump ass, giving it a squeeze. She moaned and gyrated against his palm. Ollie pulled at the fabric so that it sank into the crease of her butt, admired his handiwork for a moment, then leaned over and dragged his tongue over her slit.

"God, Ollie, I don't know how much of this I can take," she whimpered, pressing herself against the heat of his mouth. But she rolled over and laid back down, raising her arms over her head so that they touched two corners of the table.

Ollie worked quickly, fastening one wrist to one leg and doing the same for her other wrist. When he was finished, he couldn't help but step back and stare at the image before him.

Stretched out along his dining table with her long, slender legs spread-eagle and her breasts just waiting to be fondled and suckled, Leilani had never looked more beautiful. He trailed the tips of his fingers along the inside of her smooth leg and felt his cock throb at her shiver of anticipation.

"Now that you have me where you want me, what are you going to do with me?"

"I was thinking of cooling you off, actually. You're a little too hot for me." With a mischievous grin, he turned on his heel and headed for the kitchen. When he returned, he had a bucket of ice in his hand and a dangerous gleam in his eyes.

Chapter Six

Well, this has got to be the kinkiest situation I have ever gotten myself into. What was she thinking, letting this guy tie her up to his dining table? Hell, she didn't just *let* him tie her up, she even happily suggested a better way for him to do it. And now she was trussed up like a Christmas turkey and Oliver was looking at her like he wanted to swallow her whole. Maybe all the chlorine in the pool caused her to lose her damned mind. This wasn't something a decent woman did on the first date; this was something a man had to convince his woman to do after a few years of being together. It was right up there with anal sex.

The rosebud of her butt clenched involuntarily at the last thought and she had to bite her lip to keep from whimpering.

But the hunger burning in Oliver's eyes was enough to squelch the last of her doubts. This was a man who made her feel more wanted than she had ever felt in her entire life. Sure, it took a little while to convince him he wanted her more than his next gulp of air, but she was here now and about to get the fucking of her life. She hoped.

"Thank you for trusting me," he murmured, lowering his head to nuzzle her inner thighs.

Leilani felt like giggling when his day-old beard tickled her skin. "Just don't let me regret it, Ollie." She raised her hips from the cold, hard wood when he reached for the garter of her bikini bottoms and pulled them down to her thighs then dragged them all the way down her legs and past her ankles. "And you better make it worth my while."

"You're tied up on my table and still acting like a queen, huh?" He reached into the bucket of ice and plucked out one ice cube.

"You better believe it," she answered, looking warily at the ice cube in his hand.

"Hmm." He brought his hand over her body and allowed the condensation from the ice to drip on her skin. He lowered the ice to her nipple and slowly circled her areola with it, a look of utter concentration on his handsome face.

Leilani hissed through her teeth as her torso popped up from the table. "Fuck, Ollie, that's cold."

"I thought you were hot, baby. Isn't that why you snuck into my pool?" He sucked the nipple into his mouth and bit down gently before laving it with his tongue.

Her nipple, which had gone a little numb from the ice, was suddenly assaulted with sensation again as he suckled her. She couldn't help but cry out when he did it again, rubbing the ice over the nubbin until it was numb, then drawing it back into the heat of his mouth. He licked and nibbled one breast while his cold fingers plucked and pinched the nipple of the other. The alternating hot and cold drove her crazy and had her squirming on the hard table.

"Oh God," she whispered as she watched him reach into the bucket for another piece of ice. *This man is going to kill me.*

Instead of applying it to her nipples, he stroked it over her face, brushing it over her eyebrows and the bridge of her nose. Her heated cheeks welcomed the icy kisses and she moaned as he traced the shape of her lips with it. She caught a portion of it in between her teeth and drew it in along with his finger. He pulled the ice out, but returned his finger to her mouth, allowing her to suck on it. She bathed the digit with her tongue, making sure her eyes stayed on his as she sucked harder on it. With a groan, he pulled his finger out and replaced it with his tongue, plunging deep while his hand wandered back to her torso to play with her breasts.

Below her waist, her pussy wept in neglect, begging for the same attention he lavished on her tits and mouth. She wanted his tongue, his fingers, his cock down there. She didn't care; she just wanted any part of him inside her. God, if her hands were free, she would grab his hair and push his head down there.

As though he'd read her mind, he raised his head and looked deep in her eyes, his own eyes darkening until they were almost black. "What do you want, baby?" He splayed his hand across her stomach, one finger maddeningly close to the top of her mound, but not close enough. "Do you want me to suckle your breasts some more? Do you want me to lick that sweet, sweet pussy? Or do you want me to fuck you with my cock?"

She rolled her head to the side and noticed he was still wearing his red board shorts. The way his penis tented the material should have looked ridiculous, but it only made her mouth water. "God, *yes*, all of those. Please, Ollie...please take off your shorts and *fuck me*." She could hear herself begging, but no longer cared. There was nothing else in the world she wanted more than this man pumping between her legs.

A smirk curled his upper lip, but he hooked his thumbs into the waistband of his shorts and pushed them down his legs, kicking them off his ankles. His cock, which was easily eight inches and thicker than her wrist, sprang up from the nest of blond hair on his crotch and slapped up against his flat, muscled stomach. The plum-shaped head was a few shades darker than the trunk of his penis, almost purple in color. He gazed down at her and the blazing desire in his eyes made her breathless.

Suddenly, Leilani couldn't wait to get her lips around his cock.

"Give it here," she whispered hoarsely.

He indulged her by taking another step towards the table, his large brown balls swinging freely between his thighs. He wrapped one hand around the base of his penis and directed the head towards her mouth.

There was a bead of pre-cum that had escaped the slit and Leilani didn't waste time, swiping her tongue across the fat purple head. She liked the clean, salty taste of him. She even liked his smell. He really *did* smell like Ivory soap and...something else. Yes, something indefinably male. Was it gun oil? She felt like laughing even as she engulfed the head into her mouth and moaned around it.

Above her head, Ollie groaned and buried his hand in her hair, feeding her more of his cock until he hit the back of her throat, then gently pulling out. Leilani allowed him to set the pace, stretching her lips around his girth as he began to slowly saw in and out of her mouth. At one point, he got a little exuberant in his thrusting and caused her to gag. He pulled out immediately and lowered his head to brush his lips apologetically against hers.

"Mmm...now you're going to have to make that up to me," Leilani murmured as he continued to make soothing, I'm-sorry noises.

"And how do you propose I do that?"

"Well, I suppose you could let me go and let me ride your face for hours." He growled and nipped at her neck for that. "Or you could get up on this table and stab that cock into my pussy."

He chuckled and nuzzled her ear. "It's an antique table, babe. It wouldn't hold the both of us. I really don't want to end our day in the emergency room." He left her side for a moment, plucked his shorts from the floor and pulled out the keys to the handcuffs. "If you want a good, solid ride, we're gonna have to go to the bedroom." He went around to the head of the table and unlocked the cuffs, helping her up and rubbing her wrists. He pulled her to the edge of the table and wrapped her legs around his hips. "Hold on to me."

"Are we going to your bedroom?"

He gave her a crooked grin and the sight of it made Leilani's heart skip. "Hold on, sweetheart."

Leilani hugged him tightly and Ollie lifted her from the table, his hands cupping her butt to support her weight. He strode to the living room, laying her down on the couch. Leilani could only smile shyly at him as he stared at her as though he were drinking her in with his eyes. After a moment, he covered her with his body, propping his elbows on either side of her head. He brushed his lips against hers as he reached down to align his cock with her pussy.

Leilani was so wet that when the head of his penis prodded at the entrance of her vagina, it immediately swallowed it as though it had a mind of its own. She gripped the edges of the couch as Ollie began to push into her, luxuriating in the almost painful sensation of his girth stretching her. *This man is not wearing a condom, Leilani. You don't know him from Adam.* She was tempted to tell her inner voice to shut up—*God, he feels so good*—but sanity inconveniently returned. "Ollie," she panted, placing a hand on his chest. "Go put on a condom."

His eyes were glazed, unfocused when he looked up at her. "What?"

Leilani bit her lip as he paused in his entry into her body. "Con...dom, Ollie."

"Wait here." He grabbed her face between his hands, gave her a hard kiss and pulled out, eliciting a surprised gasp from her. "Be back in two seconds."

Leilani lay on her back and folded her hands over her stomach, staring listlessly at the ceiling. Thankfully, he was back in less than a minute, carrying a handful of tiny silver packets. He dropped the pile on the coffee table and proceeded to tear into one square foil with his white teeth.

"We gonna use all that?" Leilani asked with a grin.

"Gotta protect my girl." With a groan, he rolled the condom down the length of his cock, then placed his hands on her thighs to spread them apart. "You ready?"

Leilani touched the tip of her tongue to the corner of her mouth. "Yes."

Without a word, he slammed so hard into her, he robbed her of her breath. Leilani threw her head back as Ollie settled into a rhythmic pounding, his hips pistoning smoothly between her legs. Lowering his head, he buried his face in her neck, sucking her flesh into his mouth and biting down as though he meant to mark her. Leilani cried out and he began to really drive into her, hard enough that the sound of their skin slapping together reverberated throughout the living room.

Without warning, Ollie pulled out of her, turned her around and draped her over the armrest. Before Leilani could say anything, he thrust into her again, his balls slapping repeatedly against her mound. At this angle, Ollie was in her so deeply that she hysterically believed for a moment she could feel him in her throat. Leilani braced herself on the couch cushions as

Ollie hammered into her, and she found herself thrusting against him, gyrating her hips against his crotch. Ollie groaned and held her tight against his hard body, slipping his hand from her hip to her pubic bone, then down to her clit. Sucking her earlobe between his teeth, he pinched her clit between his fingers and sent her over the edge.

Leilani screamed as her orgasm slammed into her like a Mack truck. There was no build-up, no warning. It hit her so hard and so fast she actually saw stars. Her pussy squeezed like a vise-grip around Ollie's cock and suddenly, he was coming too, grunting and shuddering. He slumped against her body, but his muscular forearm on the table kept him from squishing her. They stood like that for what seemed like an eternity, their bodies slick with sweat, both of them breathing hard, and Ollie plastered to her ass like he had no intention of getting off of her. She reached behind him, cupped one taut buttock and hugged him tighter.

"Damn, girl," he breathed into her ear. "That was definitely worth the wait."

"Mmm...but now I'm all sticky." God, she loved the feeling of his body against hers, his breath on her neck. Her big, brawny warrior.

"Don't worry, babe. I'll take care of you." He pulled out of her and turned her around, placing her on her back again. Giving her one of those heartbreaking grins, he turned away and headed for the kitchen. When he returned, he had a washcloth in his hands, which he pressed between her legs. It was cool and wet against her heated skin. He spread her lips apart with his fingers and began to clean her in that efficient, careful way of his. When Leilani started rubbing herself against his hand, he gently pinched her clit and Leilani came apart.

As soon as the spasm subsided, Leilani sank bonelessly into the cushions and would have been satisfied to lay there for the rest of her life if Ollie hadn't outfitted his cock with another condom and plunged himself into her pussy again. This time, he took his time, slowly pulling himself almost all the way out, before slamming himself back in. Leilani wrapped her arms around him and allowed him to love her, kissing him deeply, savoring his masculine taste on her tongue. When she came, Ollie was thrusting into her telling her how beautiful she was. When he had his own orgasm, it pushed her over the edge again and she screamed her pleasure into his mouth.

"And we're back to sticky again," she murmured against his neck. "Wanna clean me off?"

He chuckled and nuzzled her cheek. "You're going to have to wait, babe. I'm spent." He kissed her softly and pressed his forehead to hers. "Hey, Lei?"

She smiled, loving the way her nickname sounded on his lips. She pulled back and wiped off the sweat from his eyebrow with her thumb. "Yes, Ollie?"

"I want to ask you something."

She squeezed her thighs around him and lifted her head so she could plant a kiss on his chin. "You're not going to ask me to marry you already, are you? We barely started this thing."

"Lei, this 'thing' started a month ago when you flashed your pink thong at me." He slid his hands to her waist and gave her a squeeze. "But no, baby. I'm not asking you to marry me. Not yet, at least."

As crazy as it was, Leilani almost wished he would pop the question. Looking into his beautiful green eyes, she could definitely see a future with him and for an insane second, she wanted it so badly, it actually hurt to think about it. "What is it, then?"

"I'd like to take you out sometime."

She laughed and rubbed her nose against his. "Like a dinner and a movie?"

He gazed deep into her eyes, his own eyes sparkling with mirth. "Something like that, yeah."

Leilani regarded him thoughtfully for a moment, then nodded. "All right, but on one condition."

A small knot of concern appeared between his golden eyebrows. "What?"

"You let me swim in your pool whenever I want."

"Anything you want, baby, anything you want."

And then he was kissing her again and Leilani couldn't think at all, so she simply hugged him to her and kissed him back.

About the Author

Dionne Galace writes in her pajamas with her computer on her lap and a box of Thin Mints on her side. She started writing at the age of 9 after reading a Fear Street book by R.L. Stine. She currently studies creative writing in Southern California where she also lives with her husband, whom she nightly engages in a battle royale for the TV remote control.

To learn more about Dionne, please visit www.dionnegalace.com.

Sealed With a Kiss

Lila Dubois

Dedication

For TA Chase, who kept me on schedule and encouraged me to submit this story.

And for Amanda Hitchcock and the ladies at AW Watercooler for the title help, and Ange for the best beta reading around.

Chapter One

"Now stroke, good, and again, very good." The wind carried his voice, letting it slip over the skin of her cheek, swirling in the whorls of her ears along with the cold, salted wind.

Focusing on her instructions, Helena placed the left side of her paddle in the water and pulled. The sleek orange kayak jumped over the slight wave in front of them. Thrilled by the rolling motion of moving perpendicularly over the wind-shaped waves, Helena stroked again.

The Pacific stretched out in front of her. At the horizon, still dark at this early hour, the water was grey blue, but directly against the kayak it was murky green. Behind her, Catalina Island, a busy little hub of boats and environmental research centers, crowned by the city of Avalon, sat triumphant.

When the muscles in her arms started to quiver, her biceps twitching inside the wetsuit jacket she wore, Helena turned to look over her shoulder. Behind her in the kayak's rear seat sat her guide. Dark haired and tan with sapphire blue eyes—now hidden behind sunglasses—he appeared supremely confident, as if he were the master of the waves.

When Helena signed up for the kayak lessons and tour, she'd had two options. The first option allowed her to have her own kayak, with the guide in a separate vessel. While the freedom of that appealed to her, the idea of being alone atop the world's largest ocean in a vessel that looked like shark food was terribly intimidating. Helena had opted for the double kayak, and was she ever glad she had.

"Getting tired?" Ocean asked.

Helena nodded.

"Rest your arms a minute and let me guide you."

Nodding again, Helena turned to face front. Once she was sure he could not see her face, Helena rolled her eyes and grimaced at herself. Ocean O'Brian, her guide, was not only beautiful to look at, but kind, charming and easygoing. This meant that Helena had turned into a mute idiot around him. Hot guys intimidated her. She was much more comfortable with guys who were less-than-stellar looking and quiet. Men who let her be the confident one, a role she was more accustomed to playing and one that gave her control.

At this rate, she had no idea how she would make it through the week. She had to talk to him at some point. This was only her second kayaking lesson. The first was yesterday afternoon right after she brought her car over on the ferry. Today was the first full day of her ten-day vacation/mental-health break. Working as a financial planner had its perks, mostly in the salary area, but was incredibly stressful. It was easy for some of her associates to forget the money they moved around represented years of work and savings by their clients. In school, they were taught to see it as a game, but Helena never could. In every dollar she saw someone's hopes and dreams, and took prudent care of their money. Her deliberate and cautious investment strategies pushed her up the corporate ladder. The series of promotions led to a job with fewer, more significant accounts. Increased dollar value, higher profile clients with impossible demands and an ulcer had come with the promotion.

After being treated for the ulcer, Helena had taken a stand with her boss. As a result, Helena now had a junior-level planner as her assistant and a nice ten-day vacation as a "please-don't-leave" present.

The ten-day kayak training and exploration package was something she'd seen in an outdoor-vacation magazine years ago. She'd saved the article and when this vacation came up, she'd turned right around and booked her trip. With the temperature rising inside the concrete jungle of L.A., a peaceful week on an island had sounded blissful.

"Look. Three o'clock."

Helena turned her head and scanned the ocean's surface. There, bobbing just above the wave, was a seal, his head poking out from the rolling swells. They were close enough for Helena to see his long whiskers twitch before he disappeared beneath the water.

"Was that a seal?" It was much easier to talk to him when she wasn't looking at him.

"Sure was."

"Isn't this a bit far for him to be out?" *Woo-hoo!* Two sentences in a row. By the time this was over, she might be able to actually have a conversation with the man.

"Not at all. He's probably fishing for his breakfast. Seals come into shore to lie on the rocks or under the pier when they're tired and want to rest, but they spend most of their life under the water."

"Do they ever go up on the beach?"

"Only if they're sick."

Helena scanned the horizon for more bobbing heads.

"You want to try driving again?"

Helena nodded and lifted her paddle, digging into the water. With nothing but the Pacific in front of her, it was easy to forget that there was land behind her, that there was anything in the world but the wind, water and the sun chasing the night into the western horizon.

Lost in the moment, Helena laid her paddle across her thighs. Fingers spread wide, she reached into the cold water, shivering in pleasure at its salty touch on her flesh.

Raising her hands, Helena tilted her head back, letting drops fall on her face, thanking the world for this perfect moment in the only way she could.

Ocean put one paddle in the water, controlling the roll of the kayak. Luckily the motion was automatic, prompted by years of piloting light, sleek vessels over the waves.

He was distracted by the brunette in front of him who, until this moment, had been just another client, fit and pretty, but unremarkable.

He watched, stunned, as she dipped her fingers into the water and then raised them to the sky in an offering, a prayer as primal as humanity and timeless as the ocean they sat on. She repeated the motion, her head falling farther back. The wind whipped wisps of her hair from her braid and lifted them so the sun could kiss them, turning brown to red and gold.

When she repeated the motion a ritual third time, a little ripple made its way over Ocean's skin.

Was this a sign? For her to do this so soon after they saw the seal? Did she know what he was? Was she of the sea?

She lowered her arms and picked up her paddle. He could tell from the hunch in her shoulders that she was embarrassed by what she'd done. Ocean wanted to tell her not to be embarrassed, not to doubt what had been an unpracticed and heartfelt expression of joy and thanks.

She started paddling once more, the subtle muscles in her arms flexing as she propelled them over the water. Shaking himself out of the lingering astonishment, Ocean put his paddle in the water and helped her. Something magical had just happened, and when they reached land, he intended to investigate her most thoroughly.

❧

They paddled up beside the low floating dock a few hours later. Helena nervously held onto the edge of the cold aluminum as Ocean maneuvered himself out of the back opening and onto the dock. Once he was out, the kayak started to float away. Helena, with the paddle in one hand and the other desperately trying to hold onto the edge of the slippery dock, emitted a squeak of distress.

Ocean laughed. "Don't worry, gorgeous, I've got you."

Gorgeous? Was he talking to the kayak?

He pulled the kayak up to the dock, looped a rope through the eyelet and helped Helena out. Three hours sitting in a kayak that had acquired half an inch of frigid ocean water in the bottom had atrophied the muscles in her legs and ass.

In a maneuver right out of a bad romantic comedy, the minute she tried to stand up on her own, Helena collapsed against Ocean.

"Oh no, I'm sorry. My legs are...broken or something."

He laughed. "Not to worry, gorgeous, you're just tired and a bit stiff." After making sure she could stay upright, Ocean dipped to one knee. He wrapped his hands around her right calf, working at her leg, which was bare beneath the knee-length wetsuit pants she wore.

"What are you doing?"

"Warming you up." His hands switched to her left calf, kneading and softening the muscle, before coming back to her right leg and thigh. One hand on the front, one hand on the back, he squeezed her flesh, manipulating the stiff muscles. "Feel any better?"

Helena, heart in her throat, staring dumbly at the top of his head, nodded. It took a moment for Ocean to look up, but when he did, he answered her dumbfounded expression with a quizzical one.

"Helena, if this makes you uncomfortable, please let me know."

"Uncomfortable? No, not that..."

"Can you tell me what's wrong?"

"Who says anything is wrong?"

"You're looking at me like I'm an ax murderer."

"Oh. I'm sorry, it's not that at all." Helena could have smacked herself. Why couldn't she say something intelligent instead of answering questions with questions or stuttering useless platitudes?

"Then what's wrong?"

"I'm just nervous."

"I'm making you nervous?"

"Yes."

"Like, you're nervous I'm going feed you to the sharks when we go out tomorrow morning, or you have a boyfriend named Bruno who would break both my legs if he saw me touching you?"

His head was down, focusing on working the kinks out of her legs, but his probing question made it clear that he wanted to know if she was in a relationship. Helena knotted her fingers together in nervous excitement, flattered and unnerved by his interest. She wasn't so beautiful that every man she met wanted to sleep with her, and her painful self-doubt insisted that she'd read the signals wrong.

"I don't have a Bruno, I mean boyfriend." She wished she were a better flirt, able to whip out witty banter at a moment's notice.

"Then you're worried I'll feed you to the sharks?"

"Well I wasn't, but now I'm starting to."

Ocean threw his head back and laughed, a full-bodied sound. He laughed as if he didn't care who knew he was amused. Helena smiled, his mirth infectious, her chest and cheeks flushing with pleasure at having made him laugh.

"If I promise not to feed you to the sharks"—his eyes sparkled with amusement as he said it—"will you stop looking so worried?"

"I'll try, I just get nervous talking to pretty guys."

"Pretty?" He seemed disgusted with what she'd said, though she meant it as a compliment.

"I, um, meant handsome, not pretty."

He gifted her with a tender smile, and Helena worried that she'd just changed attraction to fraternal caring with one careless comment. It wouldn't be the first time, but she felt a deep pang of sadness at having lost his interest.

"I'm glad you think I'm handsome."

"I bet girls tell you that all the time."

"Maybe." At least he had the grace to acknowledge it. "But it's not other girl's opinions that matter right now, just yours."

There was a silky quality to his voice, a bedroom smooth that overrode her earlier conclusion that he'd lost interest in her. Ocean's manipulation of her muscles changed along with his voice, from physical-therapist massage to lover's caress. He pushed to his feet, hands circling her hips and thighs in a slow, deliberate touch.

"You smell like the sea, and all I can think about is making love to you. I want to lick the smell of salt off every"—Ocean pressed his lips to her right ear—"inch"—he moved his mouth to her other ear—"of you."

Between the midday sun and him, she was more than warmed up. Protected from the wind by the raised pier, there was nothing to cool her. From above, the sun baked her inside the black wetsuit jacket and shorts she wore. Ocean's hands on her thighs pressed her against his wetsuit-clad body.

She was on vacation, her first one in a long time. A man she found attractive, if intimidating, had just made it clear he was interested in having sex with her.

Helena had two options. She could push away from him, make it clear she didn't find this behavior appropriate and continue her vacation. Or she could pretend to be someone else, a woman so confident that she had sexuality to burn and ate gorgeous men for breakfast. The second option terrified her, but the sun's heat combined with his presence and his touch burned away her reservations, questions, worries and doubts.

Helena shook her hair back, imagining it was a rich, flowing mane of blonde locks rather than a bedraggled brown braid.

"I want to feel you. I want you to touch me, taste me. I want to feel your body above mine, in mine." If her words were awkward and forced, her voice shaking in nerves, he had the grace to ignore it.

He pressed his lips against her cheek and smiled, letting her feel his pleasure. Those lips then traveled across her cheek. Helena started to turn her head into the kiss, but Ocean pulled away.

"No. I want to save that, save this kiss, until the perfect moment." His voice promised things she couldn't imagine, promised kisses that changed lives.

"Um, okay. I mean, yes, I want the perfect kiss too." Denied his kiss, she suddenly wanted nothing more in the world than his lips on hers.

"Come on, gorgeous, let's get you out of those clothes."

Chapter Two

Helena leaned her sweaty forehead against the bathroom wall. This was crazy, but it felt right, felt good. She had never had a one-night stand, or even really had casual sex. Helena wasn't a prude, but the idea had always made her feel dirty, as if the sex would be so tainted by the circumstances it wouldn't be satisfying. She had never understood fantasies about meeting a stranger, having sex with him and then walking away. For her, it came down to trust. She had to trust her lover, and trust was not something that could be had with a casual-sex partner. But, despite all these personal rules and society's warnings, she was willing and eager to sleep with Ocean because she trusted him.

It didn't have anything to do with the fact that he was gorgeous.

Ruefully amused at her own prissy justifications, Helena stripped out of the wetsuit. She was in the ladies' room in Ocean's Tours headquarters for the business. Stripped down to the swimsuit she wore underneath, Helena pulled on the sweat pants she'd worn that morning. At four a.m. when she got dressed, the sweat suit had seemed like a good idea, protection against the morning chill, but now it was simply too hot.

Tying the sleeves of the hooded sweatshirt around her waist, Helena slipped her feet into flip-flops and opened the door.

Ocean stood behind the small counter, a binder open in front of him and the phone stuck between his shoulder and ear. He wore a pair of knee-length board shorts and a T-shirt with the company logo on the back.

"Now then, did you want the full Kayak Explorer tour or did you want daily lessons?"

As he listened to the response, Helena made her way around to the front of the counter, grinning when she saw the gold wire frame glasses perched on his nose. Smiling, she leaned across the counter and touched the tip of her finger to the thin piece of wire over the bridge of his nose, the glasses making him more approachable, giving her the courage to flirt. Ocean captured her hand and slid her finger into his mouth. Helena's thigh muscles gave a quick tremble as he sucked the tip of her captured finger before turning his head and biting the pad of skin at the base of her thumb. He was clearly the better flirt.

He released her hand. "Absolutely. We can do that. I look forward to seeing you then." Eyes on her, Ocean ended the call. "Are you ready to go?"

Helena nodded, her tingling hand and the reality of what she was about to do making her mute.

Ocean scooped up a duffle bag and came around the counter, placing one hand on her back and leading her out the front door. Helena waited in the bright sunlight for him to close down and lock up the building. When he came out into the light, she was struck again by his pretty-boy looks.

He wore his dark hair long. The majority fell to his ears, cut in soft layers, allowing locks to drift forward in front of his eyes.

He ran his fingers through one side, scooping it behind his ear. Almost immediately, most of it fell forward again. In the sunlight, his hair picked up hints of russet, not the uniform black it had appeared that morning.

His eyes were blue. Ocean blue. Helena slipped her fingers into his when he held out his hand. The small hotel where Helena was staying was near the dock, probably the reason why her vacation package included accommodations there. It was not to the hotel, but to Ocean's truck, that they headed. After opening her door, Ocean slung his bag into the back and climbed in.

Helena leaned back against the seat and closed her eyes.

Ocean stuffed the key into the ignition and started the car, taking his eyes off Helena long enough to back out of the parking lot and turn onto the main road. Her eyes were closed, her head resting against the back of the seat. She might have looked relaxed if you didn't notice the faint tightness around her eyes and the nervous motion of her fingers, pleating and smoothing the fabric of her sweats. He found her nervousness adorable, her brave attempts at femme fatale endearing, but now it was time to see how much she would take, how far she would go.

"Take off your sweats."

"Why?" she asked.

"Please."

Eyes still closed, she braced her feet on the floor and lifted her hips, slipping the pants and knotted hoody down and off. She let them pool on the floorboard. Helena crossed her lightly tanned, satiny soft and smooth legs, drawing his attention to her best feature.

Hello, legs.

Ocean took in her long stems and forced himself to focus on the road, shooting glances at her out of the corner of his eye. Her suit had bikini-style bottoms but the material of the top extended down her waist to meet them, making it look like a single piece. She'd been hiding those under the clothing, but now, wearing only her bikini bottom, her secret was out.

The built-in underwire of the top hugged and lifted her breasts, offering them up for Ocean's viewing pleasure. The suit was a simple dark green with silver stitching, the color of lush leaves near a rainforest pool. Her skin glowed a pale cream in contrast.

Ocean breathed deep, keeping his attention on the road. He was a leg man, and those were a truly exemplary set. He imagined them wrapped around his body as he rode her, and nearly crashed the car. He needed to slow down. They had all day and night to play, no reason to get too excited now.

"Open your eyes," he whispered, voice rough from arousal. "Helena."

Her wide eyes had a doe-like softness to them, at odds with her flirting body language. She was beautiful, magic, utterly unique.

"All right, gorgeous, I want you to turn in your seat. Put your back against the door and swing one leg up and onto my lap. Leave the other on the floor."

In the warm cabin of the truck, Helena obeyed, turning and placing her left leg across his lap, slipping her foot between his knees and the steering wheel. She drew her other leg in close to the seat.

Ocean, eyes still on the road, wrapped his right hand around her calf and slid his palm up her leg to her thigh. Her skin was smooth under his hard palm. He pressed his fingertips into her exposed inner thigh, massaging it as he had on the dock, but this massage had no pretense of physical therapy. It was purely sexual.

Her other leg fell to the side, splaying her open, only a thin barrier of stretch fabric interrupting his view of her sex. His palm traveled back down her leg, even moving under the steering wheel so he could cup her foot, pressing his fingertips into the arch.

He pulled off the road into a parking lot. At one end a small dock stretched out, with other small docks sticking out the sides like evenly spaced tree branches, a stately sailboat docked in each slip.

Tall masts with furled sails speared up, and endless lace patterns of white ropes glittered against the blue sky.

"You live on a boat?"

"A sail boat. A thirty-one foot Catalina 310 to be precise."

"Which one is it?"

"I'll take you to meet her."

Ocean jumped out of the truck, grabbed his bag and came around to her side of the truck. He opened the door and held out a hand.

"Just a second, let me get my pants." She was blushing, trying to hide it by reaching down for her sweats.

"No, leave them."

"I can't just walk to the boat in my—"

"Yes, you can." He smiled, making it a challenge.

Helena fished her shoes out from under the sweats and slid on the flip-flops, leaving the pants behind. Her flush might have been from embarrassment, but he didn't think so. To him it looked like arousal. Placing her hand in his, she hopped out of the truck. Ocean gifted her with another smile as they passed out of the parking lot and onto the dock. Made of smooth, tight-fitting planks, it was unlike the rough and uneven boardwalk-style docks. This was a real dock, a working dock.

"So you can live on these little boats?"

"Not comfortably, no." Ocean smiled as he said it and Helena laughed. "One of the back rooms down at the office is full of my stuff. I sank my life savings into her. Someday I'll need an apartment, but for now it is just me and Moira." He gestured to their left.

Sitting calm and pretty in the green water was a sleek white lady. "Moira" was written out in navy script on the side. The sails were down, strapped to the arms by coverings.

"Your boat is very pretty." Helena's comment was cautious, as if she wasn't sure what kind of compliment was appropriate. Non-boat people were often unnerved by the personification of the vessels.

"She is, isn't she?" He loved his boat, and it was apparent in his voice. "Come on, let me introduce you."

They moved down the short pier running along the left side of the boat. Ocean moved in front of her onto the platform at the back of the boat and swung open the thigh-high door which gave access to the cockpit.

Ocean held her hand tight in his as he guided her onto the ship and through the little door. One step down had them standing in a comfortable seating area where the captain's chair was situated. Helena looked around curiously, and Ocean took advantage of her distraction to slip his hands around her waist, fingertips sneaking under the waistband to press against her bare hips.

"Helena," he whispered in her ear, "I would like you to meet Moira. Moira, this beautiful creature is Helena, who has already proven herself a lover of the ocean."

Ocean laced their fingers together once more and led her to the door to the cabin. It was blessedly cool below deck, the light maple-colored paneling and the white and navy décor giving the room a welcoming feel. The minute they stepped inside Ocean remembered he wasn't exactly ready for guests.

"Just stay here for a minute while I go clean up the berth."

"The what?"

"Bedroom."

Less than ten steps had Ocean at the door to the bedroom, which he opened a crack and squeezed in, not wanting her to see the mess inside. Helena craned her head to see past him, but Ocean slammed the door shut, leaving her in the cluttered cabin while he dealt with the truly disastrous berth.

Helena smiled as the door closed. She liked that he was messy, it made him much less perfect and the situation less surreal. She'd been suffering from regrets and nerves in the car on the way here, but they were drowned out by her arousal. Ocean made her feel beautiful, sexy. The way he looked at her did more for her self-confidence than dozens of compliments from a different man. Nothing had really happened in the truck, she was wearing a bathing suit after all, but the way he'd ordered her to strip and change position so he could play with her made it seem more sexual than some of the technical sex she'd had with previous lovers. It was almost kinky, and with him she felt sexy enough to enjoy kinky.

Pulling her braid over one shoulder, she tugged out the rubber band and fumbled to get the strands separated. Saltwater spray, like high-intensity gel, had glued the hair to itself. Grimacing at the texture, she scrubbed her fingers along her scalp.

She made her way to the low bench that wrapped along one wall of the cabin. The multitude of throw pillows made the otherwise plain seating look lush and inviting, and she plucked up a few pillows along with a faux fur throw.

Chucking the pillows to one end of the seating, she held up the blanket. It was a lopsided oval rather than square. She rubbed it against her cheek. Layers and layers of downy hair made the fur unbelievably soft. Jerking it away from her face, she curled her lip. Ugh. Not fake fur. Real fur. It seemed out of character for him to own a fur blanket, but then again, she had only known him for eighteen hours.

Resolved to talk politics *after* they had some yummy sex, she folded the blanket, and not wanting it staring at her, reached down and lifted the seat bottoms. Several of them opened but most were already full—some with essentials like canned goods and paper towels, others with life jackets and miscellaneous boat paraphernalia. When she lifted one seat to reveal a cubby full of sleeping bags, she tucked the blanket down between them. Satisfied, she made her way back to the space she had cleared, sitting and arranging herself carefully.

This was going to be fun. No, it was going to be more than fun, it was going to be hot and sexy and amazing. She wouldn't worry about her belly pudge or the fact that one boob was slightly larger than the other. She'd made a choice, the choice to have a once-in-a-lifetime vacation fling with a gorgeous man who was inexplicably attracted to her.

A smile playing over her lips, she waited for her lover.

Ocean found one last sock hidden in the folds of the sheet and stuffed it into the drawer built into the platform of the bed. As he knelt to force the overstuffed drawer closed, a dark shiver skipped down his back. A moment later, every inch of his flesh stood up in goose bumps. *His skin.*

He jerked to his feet, but could go no farther, a creepy-crawly sensation on his human skin telling him that another held his skin. Icy fear settled in his belly as his breathing became quick.

He shouldn't have left it out, or should have remembered it was just sitting there, but no one ever came on his boat, the island a tight-knit community with a low crime rate. Besides, one would have to believe in magic and faerie tales to understand the importance of his skin, and most humans had closed their minds to magic so he'd relaxed his guard.

There was only one logical culprit. Helena.

He knew she was magic, knew because she'd preformed an ocean ritual in the kayak that morning, raising the water to the sky three times. He was so entranced by this he'd never stopped to consider that her apparent knowledge of magic might mean she knew the truth about him and had come to capture him. He assumed she was of the ocean, hiding in a human skin as he was. He'd hoped to spend time with her, get to know her, and then reveal what he was, hoping his revelation would prompt her to do the same.

But now it appeared she did know what he was. Perhaps she was a witch. If so, his skin was probably gone from the boat, transported to a hiding spot by magic. Even if it were on the boat, he would have a hard time finding it.

The curse of his people dictated that once caught by others the skin would be hidden from his people's eyes. Most humans hid the skins anyway, in case the magic preventing the captured creature from seeing their skin were to fail.

His people were known to be physically beautiful and skilled lovers. That combined with the fact that once bound by the theft of their skin, his people were unwaveringly loyal to the thief, meant they were prized as husbands and wives. There had been a time when so many females had been captured, taken as loyal, beautiful wives by human men, that they'd faced extinction.

If he wanted his skin back he had only two choices. He could kill the one who had taken it. Most chose continued enslavement over committing such an act. They were creatures bound to the earth and sea. The taking of a life for anything other than food or defense was one of the most reprehensible crimes.

Or he could coax her into giving it back, please her until she returned it. Despite his nervous fear at having been trapped, he couldn't help but like the idea of coaxing his skin from her. If he chose this path he would be completely under her control, giving himself to her until she was satisfied.

The theft of a skin was powerful, uncertain magic. Having never been in this position before, Ocean couldn't know how it would affect him, or her. He needed his skin back. Knowing he could not go to the sea as long as she held it frightened him, so he forced himself not to think about it. Instead he focused on how he would get it back. This brought a smile to his face. She was shy, uncertain of her own appeal, and he wanted her. Despite the fact that she'd stolen his skin, he still wanted her. He'd been enthralled by her before she took his skin. Now they were bound by magic.

He would get his skin back, and he would enjoy doing it.

Chapter Three

When the door opened, Helena sucked in her belly, wanting to make sure she looked attractive. She sat with her long legs crossed, pillows mounded on either side of her, one hand on her thigh and the other arm stretched along the back of the bench.

He was gorgeous, just gorgeous, all dark intensity and playful charm. Her desire for him sparked uncharacteristically hard and quick, the urge to touch him so strong her fingertips tingled with it.

Ocean stood framed in the doorway, his gaze glued to her. His steps were slow and measured as he advanced toward her. The closer he got, the shorter Helena's breaths became and the tighter the knots of desire in her belly drew.

Frightened by the intensity of her reaction, Helena closed her eyes, practicing deep breathing until the inexplicably acute desire receded, leaving her feeling more like herself. Then again, maybe that was a bad idea, because when she opened her eyes Ocean was standing right next to her. The reality of him and what they were going to do had her trembling with nerves.

Ocean dropped to his knees beside her, his steady gaze moving over her. Her left leg was crossed over her right, her left foot dangling bare and vulnerable before him. He cupped her foot in both hands and pressed tender kisses to it.

Helena's mouth opened in surprise. She'd come here expecting hot sweaty sex, not tenderness.

"What will please you?" he asked.

"What, what do you mean?"

"I want to pleasure you," he whispered against the skin of her ankle.

"I, uh, I mean, I just thought we were going to have sex." His sudden intensity and odd requests were a little unnerving.

"Just sex? Is that your deepest desire?" He continued kissing her foot and ankle, giving it all the care and attention of a jeweler with a perfectly faceted diamond.

"What do you mean just sex? What were you thinking?" She tried to act cool, pretending that men worshiped her feet every day, but inside she was quivering.

Ocean shook his head at her questions and slid his hand up the inside of her left leg, lifting it so that her legs were no longer crossed. Slowly he spread her knees and inched between them. His wide palms and long fingers settled on her thighs, kneading softly.

"I want to please you, to please you more than anyone else ever has."

"Is this like, um, some kinky sex fantasy or something?" Her façade of worldly sex goddess was melting like ice cream in the sun.

Ocean growled, actually growled, in frustration. "You are of the sea. You proved that this morning. Why are you pretending you don't know what power you hold over me?"

"Power? I hold no power over you." What was he talking about?

"You do. I'm all yours, until you decide to free me."

"You are?" Was he serious or was this some sort of game? He'd changed from playful and smiling to grimly serious, and she wasn't sure she liked it.

Ocean bowed his head, and when he spoke again, his voice was tight. "What do you want? I've offered you everything, all you need to do is tell me what you want. Are you toying with me?"

Bewildered, Helena cradled his face in her hands. "I'm really not sure what you're talking about or what you want from me, but I can see I'm doing it wrong. I don't mean to make you unhappy." She hated herself for screwing this up. She should have known she wasn't cut out for this. He seemed to be playing a game that she didn't have the rules to.

He cupped her cheeks so their postures mirrored each other. "Can it be you truly don't know what you've done?" His fingers were as gentle as his voice, stroking her cheeks.

"Ocean, maybe you had better explain, because you're making me nervous."

"You have—" A hard shudder ran over his body. He took a deep breath and tried again. "The magic—" His teeth clamped closed, cutting off the last word.

"Are you okay?"

"Yes." He shook his head, then kissed her foot once more. "I was going to explain something, but I guess I can't, so we're going to stick to the original plan. All I need to be well is for you to tell me your darkest desires, let me be the canvas on which we paint your fantasies."

"Ocean, are you serious? Is this what you wanted? To, uh, know my sexual fantasies?" Helena felt like a novice swimmer who'd decided to tackle the English Channel. She was trying to understand, to play along, but felt woefully out of her depth.

"Yes, we will play them together, you and I. In that way, I will please you."

His words sent a shiver of longing down her spine. What he was offering was her greatest fantasy, a lover who would experiment with her, play with her, let her try every dark desire of her heart.

When she didn't answer he asked, "Are you embarrassed to share these fantasies with me?"

"Well, yes."

"Why?"

"Because fantasies are private things." Her protests were growing weaker. She wanted what he was offering, wanted it like a dieter wants chocolate, but years of personal reserve kept her protesting long past the time when there was any truth to her protests. She wanted him to coax it from her so that she could maintain some distance from her fantasies.

"Some are, but others are meant to be played out, meant to be lived. I want to know those."

Helena could feel the flush on her cheeks and chest. "Maybe, but we did just meet..." Sex was one thing, admitting she wanted to be spanked was another.

"I understand." Ocean rose and pulled out a drawer refrigerator in the galley opposite the seating arrangement. Taking out a half-full bottle of white wine, he poured a glass.

Helena had closed her legs when he stood, so Ocean knelt beside her, offering up the glass. She smiled in true amusement at him.

"Do you really think one glass of wine is going to get me to admit that...?"

"Yes?"

"Never mind."

"Drink then, please."

"Aren't you going to have any?" she asked between sips.

"No."

"I don't want to drink alone. You should have some too."

As if he were a marionette wielded by a clumsy puppeteer, Ocean clambered to his feet and jerked over to the wine bottle, the neck of the bottle clacking against the glass as he poured. When he returned to her side and dropped to his knees, Helena looked down at him in alarm.

"Are you okay?"

"Yes, I just didn't know what it would be like if you ordered..."

"Ocean, please, you're starting to scare me a little. Are you sure you're okay?"

"I am. I will be."

When Ocean's hand came around the back of her neck, Helena jumped a little, but he only massaged her. Now that they were quiet, she could hear the ocean, could smell the salt of their skin. Ever so slowly, her head tipped forward, allowing him access to her shoulders. Her eyes drooped closed. Beside her, she felt him shift, and moved easily when he laid her down on her belly. Placing her glass of wine on the floor, she sighed as his fingers began to dig into the muscles of her back.

"Tell me, gorgeous, what dark secrets you keep."

The sweet tingle of wine and the smell of sun and salt aroused her, the warm kiss of his voice lulled her and her own longings seduced her, and she gave in to his desire for him and what he offered.

"I've fantasized about almost everything," she admitted in a rush.

"Positions? Toys?"

"Yes and yes. The most exiting thing that has happened to me is sex in a shower, and even that wasn't good because I was worried we would slip and fall."

"If you want to have sex in water, I'll take you into the ocean, holding you there so the waves force your body onto mine, and every inch of your skin is caressed by the water. When I thrust, you will take the ocean into you."

Helena could not, would not stop the small moan that escaped her at his words.

"You would like that?"

"Oh yes."

"What else? Tell me."

"Spanking. I've always wanted to be spanked, but it seems so silly to say out loud, and I'm too tall. I wouldn't fit on a man's lap."

Ocean's hands had been kneading along her ribs, but now they slid to her ass. He dug his knuckles in, working the muscles, before cupping the globes in his hands.

"You will fit over my lap." He hooked his fingers in the waistband of her suit. "And you will take your punishment"—he pulled her suit down, exposing her bottom but not removing it—"like a good girl."

Helena's breath sped up, and she let out an excited little yelp as his bare hands settled on her ass.

"That is one fantasy, gorgeous, are there others?"

Helena knew she should keep quiet, knew that if she got to live out even one fantasy with this man it would be delicious, but the touch of his hands and the silk of his voice made her crave more, made her greedy for it.

"I always wanted to, you know, in public."

"Have sex in public?"

"Not exactly. I wanted to show myself off, or have someone show me off, to make other people want me."

"Hmmm, then you will be naked on deck. You will sunbathe naked and show off this creamy flesh for any and all who walk by."

"But it's illegal, we might get—"

"No, we won't, and yes, you will."

≃

"Take off the top."

"But someone might see," Helena protested.

"I know. Do it."

Helena slid the straps off her shoulders and pulled her arms free, her eagerness belying her protests. The suit still clung to her, tight and compressing around her breasts.

"I won't tell you again."

Breathing hard, the hot salt air rough in her lungs, she curled her fingers over the top of the suit and pushed it down. Her breasts popped free, her nipples puckered from arousal and the scrape of fabric over the pink peaks.

"Good. Now the rest."

With a surreptitious look around, Helena hooked her thumbs in the suit once again and wiggled it down her body, catching the bottoms and pulling them off at the same time. She reveled in this forbidden action, in the dark pleasure of knowing that at any time someone could come along and see her, all of her, know the secrets of her body and maybe even long for her, want to touch and caress her.

She was pulled from her reverie by Ocean's hand on her cheek. She straightened, unashamedly naked before him.

"Sometimes a fantasy isn't what we would have hoped, and is too frightening to be lived. If this isn't truly what you want, if this isn't what will please you best, then let us go below to act out one of your other desires." He was giving her an out, making sure she was okay with what was happening. She was absurdly grateful for that, as it bolstered her courage.

"This"—she stretched, arching her body back, feeling the sun along every inch of skin—"is exactly what I want."

"Good." Ocean took a definitive step back and looked her over. So lost was she in the spell of what he was doing, of what they were doing, that she forgot how self-conscious she was about her body. The fears and doubts which normally crippled her and made the first undressing with a new partner torturous were absent.

"Your belly and breasts are fair."

"That's because I keep them covered up outside."

"That must be remedied." Ocean moved past her and came back a moment later with a large beach towel, which he spread out near the prow.

Hips swaying, body slick with proof of her arousal, Helena stretched herself out on the towel. Lying on her back, she rested one arm over her eyes and let the other stretch out beside her. Her legs naturally fell open and the cool wind off the water touched her sex, which was so swollen and wet that the labia had parted.

Startled, Helena crossed her legs, hiding herself. *No.* She would not hide herself. Slowly and deliberately, she uncrossed her legs, even spreading them slightly.

She felt the thud of footsteps as Ocean moved up beside her.

"Are you comfortable?" His voice was warm and rich and perfect.

"Yes."

He lifted her arm away from her face and slid a pair of dark sunglasses onto her nose. "You're beautiful."

"Yes." With him she was, the sincerity of his voice making her believe it, if only as part of the fantasy.

Ocean stretched out beside her, propped on one arm. The sun beat down and sweat dewed on her skin. Her nipples relaxed into full pink circles.

A new voice broke into their peaceful sunbathing. "Oh my God, Ocean. Look at what you have."

Helena learned in that instant that "my heart stopped" was more than just a phrase.

"Lucky boy," a second voice called out.

Helena jerked upright, heart restarting with a painful thud, and peered through the dark glasses at the two men standing on the dock.

"Hello, lovely. My goodness, look at that hair color. I would just die for those highlights."

It took Helena a moment to realize the well-dressed gentlemen ogling her were probably not all that interested in her as a sex object.

"Mark, Jon," Ocean responded easily, his eyes still focused on her breasts. There was an awkward pause as Helena, Mark and Jon all waited for him to perform introductions.

"Stop staring at me and introduce us," she hissed at him. "Oh my God, I am naked." Her clothes were out of reach, so she settled for drawing her knees up and wrapping her arms around them.

With an odd growling noise, Ocean turned to look at Mark and Jon. "Gentlemen, this is Helena. Helena, meet Mark and Jon. They own the pretty lady across the way." He nodded at the ship with blue sails docked across from them.

"Only woman I've ever been inside," one quipped.

That startled a laugh out of Helena.

"Now if only our pretty Ocean were sunbathing with you." Mark sighed.

"Darling girl, you really shouldn't let him talk you into putting on a show unless he is going to also," John added.

Helena smiled. "I'm glad you think I'm enough to be a show."

"Of course, look at that. I even glimpsed some pussy and it actually looked nice."

Men I don't know are talking about my vagina, and I am turned on by it.

"Thank you, and you're right. Maybe Ocean should strip too."

Beside her, Ocean smiled, but it was pained. "Those two have been trying to get me naked since we met."

"Damn right," John shouted.

"Well, why don't you oblige them?" Helena grinned as she said it. Ocean looked at her, full-blown panic in his eyes.

He leaned closer and whispered in her ear. "We have a problem. I'm hard from looking at you."

His words made Helena tingle all over. "I'm glad."

"It means if you force me to strip, they will really get a show."

His use of the word force startled her, turning it from something sexy to something degrading. "I was just teasing."

227

"If you want me to, I'll strip."

"Ocean, don't be silly, if you don't want to, nothing I say will make you—"

"I will if you really want me to."

Helena leaned away. "Clearly you don't, so why say you will?"

"To please you."

Helena was losing track of the times he had said this. It was time to test their game. "Stand up."

Ocean rose immediately at her order, the muscles in his jaw clenching as he stared out at the horizon.

"Take off your shirt." Helena spoke loud enough for the men on the dock to hear.

"Oh blessed day, what is this? Can it be I finally get to see more of Mr. Ocean? Jon, are you seeing this?"

"Shhh, you're distracting me."

Ocean grabbed the back of his shirt and pulled it off.

"Throw it in the water." Helena's voice was strong and sure. The nervous, unsure stuttering gone. Either he had truly been duped and her innocence and hesitant manner were all an act, a façade to cover the fact that she was an evil witch bent on enslaving him, or the magic of the skin was working on her too.

Contact with a skin, even if it was only for a moment, brought out hidden strengths in those who touched it. When human storytellers spoke of his people, they attributed the newfound virtues and strengths of the one who'd captured the skin to the surge of confidence brought on by possessing a beautiful lover. They did not know that the skin itself had power and worked that magic on anyone who had exposure to it.

Helena was growing bolder, more confident, less bound by worries of what others would think of her.

He tossed his shirt, the fabric floating gently on the surface of the ocean.

"Come here."

Ocean stepped closer to Helena.

"Do you trust me?" she asked.

He did...and he didn't. He still didn't know what she was or why she'd taken his skin. But he wanted her, craved her, and believed that her desire for him was real also. He didn't yet fully trust her as a person, but as a lover he did. "I will do what it takes to please you."

"I don't understand you, Ocean, but I want to please you too." She rested one hand on his thigh. "I don't want you to do something you're uncomfortable with, even if it would please me best. I want you to trust me, the same way I trust you."

Looking down at her adorably earnest face, he could not bring himself to believe she was a witch. He smiled down at her and she relaxed, gifting him with a wicked grin, the magic of his skin bringing the hidden sex kitten to the surface.

"Face me, stand in front of me." Bare-chested and barefoot, he did as she ordered, his legs on either side of hers. Helena held out her hands. Hesitantly, Ocean grabbed them, bracing her as she slid her legs out from between his and curled them under herself so she was kneeling.

"My God, you wicked girl. I hope you are about to do what I think you are about to do," Mark said.

She carefully undid the laces of his board shorts, and when the waistband was loosened, eased them down. Ocean sucked in a breath as she freed his cock. He watched her examine him, her rapid breathing betraying her excitement. She moistened her lips with her tongue and he imagined his cock in her mouth, the fantasy vivid and pungent.

Helena placed her hands on his naked hips.

"Please," he whispered.

"Please what?" Her fingers made soft circles on his flesh. "Please what?" she asked again.

Helpless, Ocean just shook his head. Helena leaned in and blew across the tip of his cock. "Tell me, Ocean. Answer me." The magic worked them, pushing them into roles of dominant and submissive, not imposing on their will, merely magnifying inclinations that were already there.

At her order his words escaped him in a rush of barely formed thoughts and desires. "Please touch me, please tease me. Please put your hands on my ass and stroke my balls and play with my cock and put it in your hot mouth and please don't show them my cock or let them watch if you are going to suck me but please keep playing with me."

Ocean stumbled to silence. The magic was growing stronger, her orders more powerful, his desire to obey them more pronounced. Helena slid her hands from his hips back around to grab his ass. She dug her fingers in and the men on the dock cheered and whistled. Helena leaned to the side, brushing his cock along her cheek. The tip buried in the softness of her hair, and she licked the sensitive flesh of his belly. He jerked in her hold, his hands fisted at his sides, body ridged with excitement. Helena tightened her fingers on his ass and then pulled, separating the cheeks, exposing him, making him vulnerable as she turned her head to the side and blew on his cock. Her breath was hot and wet, a torturously delicate touch.

Though she'd barely touched him, Ocean was ready to explode. He wanted to be in her, now. As if she agreed, Helena pulled his shorts up and fastened them loosely.

"You cruel bitch. To take him away just as you were getting to the good part."

Helena grabbed Ocean's arm and pulled herself up. "Sorry, boys. He's mine."

With a cheerful smile at them, Helena slid her hand down his arm, lacing their fingers together, and led the way from the deck into the cabin. After the glaring bright light and oppressive heat, the dark interior felt like a liquid cool embrace. Here the sun's harsh rays were filtered through a large skylight and the cool colors soothed after the harsh white of topside.

Helena dropped his arm, brow furrowing in worry.

"I hope what I did up there wasn't too much." This was the real Helena shining through the magic.

"Did it please you?" he asked, wondering if the spell had somehow made her do something she didn't want.

"That's not the point."

"It is the point. The only point."

"What would please *me* is for you to tell me if what I did up there was too much. Did I upset you?" She seemed truly worried, fingers twisting together in front of her.

Ocean smiled, easing her worry. "No. It felt good, dirty."

"It did, didn't it." She blushed as she admitted this, her skin glowing from the recent brush with the sun.

For him one of the most arousing parts of the whole episode had been her genuine concern for what he wanted. "I told you what I didn't want and you didn't do it, despite knowing you have the power to force me."

"As much as we seem to be playing that I'm the dominant party, I think we both know that I couldn't make you do anything you don't wish."

Ocean simply shook his head, shifting from foot to foot. As he did, the loosely tied shorts gave up their hold and slid down to his knees. Without a word, he stepped out of them and reached for her. When his fingers brushed her arm, the slow smolder of their joint arousal erupted into flame.

His hands curled tight and bruising around her, one on her neck and the other across her shoulders. Her hands tangled in his hair. Between them, his cock felt hot and large, its stiff length pressing into her soft belly.

Ocean's lips had gone to her throat, pressing frantic kisses there, but now he pressed his lips to hers. In contrast to the harsh and needy holds they had on one another, the kiss was gentle and hesitant. Only after their mouths became softly acquainted did he change the kiss, put strength and desire into it, forcing her head back as his tongue eased between her teeth, demanding entrance to her body.

"I want you," he moaned against her throat. "I want you here and now and hard."

"Yes. Yes. Do it now."

Ocean pushed Helena up against a wall, her order turning his desire into a compulsion.

"Legs," he demanded, wrapping them around his waist when she lifted them. "Protection?" he belatedly asked.

"I'm on the pill, and I'm clean."

"Me too." He also wasn't human, and couldn't contract human diseases.

Shifting his grip higher up her thighs, he slammed inside her.

If Helena'd been any less aroused, any drier, it would have hurt her. As it was the thrust had buried him so completely that Ocean shivered in pleasure.

Hands on her ass, Ocean leaned his forehead against the wall beside her, frowning as a faint voice echoed in his head. Was it possible that...

Chapter Four

Pinned to the wall, Helena waited for him to start thrusting, but he just held her and breathed.

His head lifted from the wall. "I can hear you."

"Huh?" Why was he talking at a time like this?

"I can hear you."

"You couldn't hear me before?" If he had hearing problems, later would be a good time to discuss them. Now would be a good time for fucking.

Ocean's face had been pale, almost stunned, but now the coloring came back and he grinned, a truly wicked grin. "Whatever you are now, you were of the ocean at some point."

"Ocean, what are you—?"

Lightning fast, he withdrew and slammed into her again.

"Oh my—"

And again he slammed into her. Beyond speech, Helena dug her fingers into his shoulders, her thigh muscles tight against his hips.

Please don't stop, don't slow down, make me feel that you would die without me.

Again and again, his body rocked into hers. The rhythm was slower than the jackhammer thrusts most men degenerated into and each stroke rubbed her in all the right places.

Helena felt her orgasm condensing in her belly, like a pot beginning to boil or a wave building deep in the ocean. As it grew, Helena's head thrashed side to side. She was near frantic with it.

"Hold on," Ocean whispered, placing his head alongside hers to stop her frantic thrashing. Wild and terribly aroused, Helena turned her face into his neck, panting into his sweaty flesh as his thrusts pressed her sweat-slicked back against the wall.

Once, twice, and on the third stroke the wave broke. Helena threw her head back and gritted her teeth as an orgasm so profound it was painful racked her body. She was used to the small flutterings from vibrator-induced orgasms. This was the same sensation magnified a thousand times. She clutched around his cock so hard he stilled within her, allowing her clenching body to feed upon him.

Just when she felt it would end, felt it would subside, Ocean jerked out of her, hitched her quivering body higher on the wall and slammed into her a final time.

Helena screamed.

℘

Several eons later, Helena roused herself enough to look around. She was stretched out on the bench seating. Ocean was nowhere in sight. Helena inched to the edge of the bench and looked over. Ocean's big body was sprawled on the floor.

"You alive?"

Ocean grunted in response.

"I think I might be dead," Helena confessed, her voice thick with lazy satisfaction.

"I thought for a second you were." His voice was muffled by the carpet, his face squashed against the floor.

"That orgasm was so good that I passed out." Helena steadied her head on one hand and marveled. "I seriously passed out. I mean, I've read about that happening, but I always figured it happed to people who did Tantric sex or something like that."

"No Tantric sex here."

"You must be some sort of sex god."

"Or sex slave."

"Huh?"

"Never mind." Ocean finally shifted, sitting up and propping his back against the bench. "Are you hungry?"

"Embarrassingly so."

"Don't be embarrassed. We burned a ton of calories and we need fuel."

"I'll help you cook."

"I'm too tired to cook." With that, Ocean crawled across the floor and rummaged through the pocket of his duffle bag. His position on hands and knees gave her a truly lovely view of his nicely toned ass. If the angle were a little bit different, she might be able to see what hung between the muscled thighs.

"For the love of God, woman, give me a minute."

"What? Oh no, please tell me I didn't say that out loud."

"About my tight ass and wanting to see my poor abused cock? Yeah, I heard that."

Helena pressed her face into a pillow. She'd always been a post-sex chatterer. Apparently really good sex only made her more loquacious.

There was a thunk as Ocean resumed his place on the floor with his back against the bench. Helena unburied her face to watch him dial. From this angle, she had a quarter view of his profile. The square edge of his jaw and soft fringe of his lashes made him seem both capable and vulnerable.

Ocean's hand lifted and, without looking, he reached over his shoulder and stroked her cheek. The gesture was so tender that Helena felt almost teary. She didn't expect to be treated tenderly by the man who had just fucked her into a coma. Bitter experience had taught her men saw women as either saints or whores. If they labeled you a saint, any expression of sexual need was seen as dirty and wrong. If you were labeled a whore, you couldn't expect any tenderness or sweetness from them and expressing a desire for those things was usually met with derision. With a trembling heart and terrifyingly exposed emotions, Helena turned and pressed her lips to his fingers. He pressed back slightly, stroking her lower lip with one finger, and then withdrew his hand.

When Ocean ended the call, Helena realized she hadn't heard what he said.

"Er, what did you just do? Sorry, I spaced out for a while."

"I just ordered pizza."

"Yum, but not exactly great for you."

"Please tell me you aren't also a health-food junkie." He turned to look at her. "A stress puppy and a health-food junkie, oh the horror. I might have to toss you overboard."

"I am not a stress puppy and I am just watching my weight."

"Not another one. All you girls have fallen for Hollywood's hype about your body. You, gorgeous, have a rockin' body."

"Thanks, but I could—"

"Enough." He kissed her. "You are gorgeous. Anything you say that implies otherwise will earn you a spanking."

Helena shivered in arousal and Ocean grinned. When he leaned in, Helena turned her head, expecting a kiss, but Ocean veered away to whisper in her ear. "I just want you to know that I am going to spank you anyway. I'm going to take your long lean body and turn it over my knee, because you are such a naughty girl."

Helena bit her lower lip and closed her eyes as her imagination took the information and ran wild. Lips still near her ear, Ocean chuckled. "Gotcha."

Slowly, and with an exaggerated groan, Ocean got to his feet. Helena sat up, glad she was not a guy so her sudden arousal was easy to hide. Then again, she was getting a sneaking feeling Ocean knew what she wanted and wouldn't be fooled by her pretense.

"So, gorgeous, what is it you do that has turned you into such a stress puppy?" Ocean held out a hand and pulled her up. Trying to appear unembarrassed by her nakedness—which seemed woefully late in arriving considering her public display earlier—Helena answered. She explained her job as Ocean found a T-shirt for her to wear, handing it to her as they took turns using the small bathroom.

Thirty minutes later, a loud whistle had Ocean going topside wearing the board shorts he had pulled on. He returned with an extra large pizza and a pack of Coke. They dug in, comfortably seated at the small, built-in dinette. The topic moved from her work to his and Ocean soon had her in stitches with the antics of some of his clients. By the time they finished, it was midafternoon and they decided to go topside for more sunbathing.

Before they moved topside, Ocean pulled her T-shirt off. On deck, Ocean spread out a beach towel for her. The strange sexual confidence of a few hours ago returned and Helena shot Ocean a seductive smile as she made her way to the blanket. There she stretched out on her back, arms above her head, one knee bent, coyly hiding her sex.

Ocean lay face down beside her, and for several moments they simply basked in the sun like the sated beasts they were.

"Oh no, I forgot sunscreen." Helena sat up, peering at Ocean through the dark glasses he provided. "Do you have any?"

He opened one eye and gave her a slow once-over. "I'll get some."

Helena lay back and waited. When Ocean returned, there was a thickness to the air around him, and the tense set to his shoulders told her their play was about to begin again.

Ocean straddled her hips, forcing her bent knee flat. "Give me your right arm."

Helena lifted and extended her arm as Ocean poured sunscreen into his palm. Helena shivered as he placed hands coated in cool sunscreen on her wrist. From wrist to shoulder, he worked the lotion into her skin, the scent of coconut strong in the heated air.

When he finished, Ocean carefully replaced her arm in its position above her head and started in on the other, giving it the same treatment.

He left no part of her body unattended, swiping fingers over her cheeks, nose and forehead, kneading her upper chest, causing her to squirm as he massaged her ticklish belly.

239

When every inch of skin above her waist was covered, save her breasts, Ocean leaned down and blew on her nipples. His breath, like the air around them, was hot and so had no effect. With a disapproving noise, Ocean grabbed the bottle of sunscreen. Holding it upside down, he squeezed and a large dollop of the still-cold cream landed right on her nipple.

Helena yelped. The sound cut off as he gave the other peak the same treatment.

One large palm covered each breast, pressing the cold into her skin. Her nipples beaded up hard and Ocean rumbled with pleasure. His fingers slid through the creamy pools melting down her breasts and plucked on the hard buds.

"Oh yes, yes, yes. Do that again."

Ocean obeyed, pinching the flesh between his fingers and lifting. Coated as they were, the pebbled tips slid through his fingers, forced between the viselike pressure of his fingertips. When first the right and then the left peak finally slid from his grip with a pinch, Helena moaned in pleasure, her fingers wrapped around his forearms, nails digging into him.

Slowly he worked the sunscreen into her breasts, kneading the soft mounds, molding and shaping them with hands rough from his work. When the lotion was gone, he repeated the nipple pinch, the hold now lasting longer as her body had absorbed much of the sunscreen. As he squeezed hard and lifted her breasts away from her body by their tender peaks, Helena's hips moved helplessly beneath Ocean.

"Ah, ah, ah, gorgeous, stay still, I'll be down there soon."

Beyond words, Helena nodded, her hips stilling as her nipples slipped free of his pinching grip.

Ocean flipped around, still straddling her belly, presenting her with a view of his wide golden back. Hands once more filled with sunscreen lifted each leg, working the lotion into her skin, not missing one inch, from the soles of her feet to the outside of her hips. As he lowered her legs he bent them at the knee, so when he was done they fell open, mercilessly exposing her sex.

Please, touch me, she thought, *touch me and please me and make me whole. Make it dirty and sweet and lovely.*

Ocean finished smoothing lotion up the inside of her thighs. His hands inched closer and closer to her sex.

Finally he placed four fingertips along each lip of her sex and carefully separated them, exposing her soft pink core.

"Your pussy is gorgeous. Just like you."

Helena gulped. She had never had a man talk about her sex, at least in any direct manner.

"It is true. The lips are nice and long, and when you are aroused, like you are right now, they puff up fat and pink, inviting me to explore." The fingers near the top of her sex pulled a little bit more, opening her up wider at the top. "And there's my pretty girl. Your clit is beautiful, a thing of artistry. I haven't even touched her yet and she is poking out of the hood to see me."

Helena slid her hands up and down his back as he spoke, wanting him to know how much she was enjoying his words.

Ocean continued to verbally love her sex as if he knew what her caressing hand meant.

"You are all deep pink inside with a soft pearl white cream. Your body is ready for mine again, calling out to me."

Changing his hold, Ocean now kept her sex open with the index and middle finger of one hand, leaving the other hand free to explore her depths.

"I want you to clench, show me how wet and ready you are. Yes, that's it, good girl. Now stay clenched tight while I work my finger inside you."

Helena dug her nails into his back as her sex squeezed tight. Her heart was pounding so loud in her head that she almost couldn't hear him. Later, she would be embarrassed, but right now her molten arousal burned away any thoughts of embarrassment.

"Good, good. Oh yeah. Gorgeous, you are perfect, soft and wet and hot. You are so tight and pretty like this. Can you feel me inside you? I think you can. Do you want me to touch your clit?"

She lifted her hips, telling him without words that she did, she did want him to touch her.

"No, no. I won't let you get away with that. Do you want me to touch your clit?"

Helena rubbed her hands on his back. She didn't want to talk, afraid that the sound of her voice, her plain, familiar voice, would break the spell woven by his deep, dark words.

Ocean gave one of her labia a punishing pinch. "Answer me, gorgeous."

"Yes, yes, I want you to touch my clit." She rushed the words out, her voice breathy and deep, different enough from her normal speaking voice that she could almost imagine it was not her talking, but some confident and secure woman.

"Tell me how."

"I want you to stroke it and lick it and...and maybe pinch it."

"Good girl."

She watched his torso descend, felt the rush of his breath against her wet sex, and then his tongue was on her, lapping her clit. His fingers kept her sex spread wide so his tongue found no hindrance as it traveled from her clit to her entrance and back again. The touch was soft and encompassing, each stroke swiping every inch.

He pulled back and Helena followed him with her hips, pushing up against the cage of his legs.

"More, more, more."

His face descended immediately and she could feel him smiling against the inside of her sex. "As my lady commands."

His lips took her clit between them and pressed gently. Helena sighed. With any other man she would have feared he would stop too soon and leave her unsatisfied, but Ocean would not. She let herself relax into the sensation.

With her clit surrounded by his lips, he stroked the little captured peak with the tip of his tongue. The touch was precise, the nerve endings so overwhelmed that her thigh muscles quivered and Helena bit her lower lip in response.

She was close, so close, just a bit harder sensation and she would—

Ocean slid the index and middle finger of each hand into her, filling her with four of his strong, thick digits. Helena yelped at the sudden invasion and then moaned.

It was the best of everything to have her sex so completely full and her clit so perfectly licked. His tongue kept up its relentless and precise assault, the rhythm never varying, making sure the orgasm built but never peaked. She was in stasis, dangling off a precipice, held between falling and flight by his command and her desire.

Then it happened. His lips were replaced by his teeth, biting into her clit, the pain turned to pleasure by the ferocity of her orgasm.

Nails sunk deep into his back, Helena screamed her satisfaction to the sky.

Chapter Five

"Helena. Gorgeous, I'm starting to worry. Wake up."

There was a soft touch against her face and then something moved inside her sex. Helena opened her eyes with a sigh of residual pleasure.

"You...made...me...pass out...again."

"Gorgeous, I am convinced it has more to do with the strength of your passion than it does with me."

"Nuh-uh, you...amazing."

"I just know what you like." Ocean still had two fingers inside her and he slowly thrust them in and out of her orgasm-tight sex. Helena felt her eyes roll back in her head as her hips lifted in response.

"You're practically a mind reader." She gasped.

Ocean turned his head sharply to look at her, his smiling face gone serious. Uncomfortable at his close scrutiny, she wiggled her hips, planning to move away, but he hooked his fingers inside her, holding her still.

With a sigh, his face softened and he leaned down for a kiss. Confused and worried about the look he'd given her, Moira kept her lips unmoving against his. He gentled her with pecks on the corners of her lips and the tip of her nose, even rubbing his nose against hers in a cold weather kiss. Helena

244

remembered the Eskimo kiss from her childhood and when she smiled at the memory, he took her lips again. This time she allowed him entrance, his tongue tasting the space between her bottom lip and teeth. She sighed into his mouth and he breathed in, and when his breath escaped into her, she willingly took it in, sharing the air.

His fingers slipped out of her with a parting rub to her clit, and Helena bit down on his lower lip.

"Like that?" Ocean asked.

"Yes, but I'm a little sore."

"I hope you're not too sore. Remember what I said comes next."

Her breath hitched. "A spanking."

He kissed her shoulder. "Among other things." Leaning up on one elbow, he smiled at her. "Do you realize you just had a screaming orgasm outside where anyone could see?"

With a jolt, Helena looked at the darkening sky, the dock, the other boats and the sea beyond, which appeared orange in the light of the now-setting sun. Wide-eyed, she turned to Ocean, who threw his head back and roared with laughter.

"Shhhh!" As Ocean rolled onto his back, Helena scrambled after him, slapping her hand over his mouth and pressing herself up against his side to hide her nakedness. Ocean's laughter, now silent, was a rumble in his chest.

"I am so embarrassed."

Ocean took her hand and kissed the palm. "No you're not."

"Yes, I am!"

"No, my gorgeous exhibitionist. You are not."

Helena tucked her head to hide her smile. He was right. Her initial horror was more of a conditioned response than any true embarrassment. "I've never been like this before."

"It doesn't matter. Today is about you and what will please you best."

"Someday will you tell me why you keep saying that?"

Ocean kissed her wrist again but said no more.

⃰ ℧

Freshly scrubbed and wearing one of Ocean's T-shirts, Helena sat on the bench, waiting for Ocean to get out of the shower. She felt like a sated beast. She was aware of muscles in her legs, lower abdomen and groin that had not been exercised in an embarrassingly long time.

Her body was loose from the orgasms and she felt very well loved.

Loved.

During that last orgasm, in the pure moment of freedom it provided, some small part of her marveled that she trusted this man enough to let go completely. The way he touched her spoke to her in a way she had not known before.

Their affair should be nothing more than a vacation fling between consenting adults with minimal true emotional involvement, but he'd kissed her like he meant it.

She wanted to know everything about him. Did he have any brothers or sisters? What were his favorite color, food, movie and band? Chocolate chip or oatmeal cookies? She hoped it was oatmeal as she had a great oatmeal cookie recipe she could make for him. What did he look like when he slept and did he wake up fast or slow?

Hugging her knees to her chest, Helena tried to suppress the emotions prompting the curiosity. She was a grown woman;

she could have sex without falling in love. But that was what this felt like. Love.

Disgusted with herself, Helena pressed her forehead hard into her upraised knees. Great sex coupled with tenderness and she was in love. Was she really so simple?

After all, what did she know about Ocean? So many things he did and said were mysteries.

But as much as she fought it, there was a lightness in her heart, a quick trip of anticipation every time she thought of him. For God's sake, she was thinking of baking for him. She wondered if the feminist majority would kick her out for losing her cool.

It couldn't be helped. She'd fallen in love.

"You okay, gorgeous?" Ocean stood outside the bathroom door, a towel around his waist. She wanted to lick the water drop from his chest.

"Helena... Helena? Are you there?"

"Hmmm?"

"Daydreaming?"

"Dreaming of something."

"Are you flirting with me?"

"I'm trying."

He walked over and kissed her lightly. "You're succeeding. But I thought you were too sore and that's why I had to shower alone."

Pretending a blush wasn't heating her cheeks, she responded, "I am sore, but flirting is fun."

"Flirting can get naughty girls into trouble."

Helena shivered.

"But first I think we need to eat again. How do you feel about cold pizza?"

"I love it."

"You may turn out to be the perfect woman."

Standing at the small counter, they ate cold pizza out of the box, silent but for gentle teasing about inconsequential things. Belly full, Helena felt drowsy and longed for a quick nap. Setting down the half a slice of pizza she held, she moved against Ocean. He unhesitatingly opened his arm to tuck her against his side so she could rest her head on his shoulder. Closing her eyes, she drifted, soaking up this companionable touch with as much pleasure as she had the lover's touch.

When he finished, he guided them to the bench seating.

"Bed," Helena mumbled.

"Hmm?"

"Want bed."

"I'm saving that."

"M'kay."

Ocean arranged pillows so he could lean back against the armrest at the end of the seating arrangement. Once he was in place, he pulled Helena down on top of him, front to front, her head pillowed on his chest, his arms around her.

Rubbing her cheek on his skin, which smelled of soap and ocean, Helena closed her eyes and willed herself to just breathe, to just *be*. She loved him, and in this moment, secure in his tender arms, she could believe he loved her too.

ૹ

Hours later Helena woke with a shiver. She didn't know how long she'd been asleep but her internal clock said it was late, past midnight. When she shivered again, Helena realized the cold had woken her. She still lay cradled against Ocean's chest, but now one of his arms was flung above his head and the other dangled at his side, leaving her without the warmth of his embrace.

Still misty eyed with sleep, even as goose bumps dotted the skin of her legs, Helena crawled down the bench, searching for the compartment where she had stored the little blanket. Carefully and as quietly as possible, she lifted the seats, finding the right compartment on her third try.

Reaching down into the dark, she felt around for the blanket. She stifled a yelp as her hand pressed against something soft and *warm*. Helena retracted her hand and took a deep breath. That was impossible. It was cold in the boat, situated as it was on top of the water, and the nylon sleeping bags the throw was stuffed between had both been cool to the touch. Shaking her head at her own foolishness, Helena reached in again and pulled out the throw before she could analyze its disturbing warmth.

Crawling backwards, she snuggled down against Ocean's chest once more. When he moved restlessly, Helena tugged the blanket farther up, covering the portion of his chest she wasn't lying on.

Quick as a snake strike, Ocean seized the throw from her, ripping it from her and sliding from beneath her.

"Ocean, what—?"

Ocean wrapped the hand not holding the blanket around her arm, fingers digging in painfully, dragging her up.

"You touched the skin to me, I am free of you." Ocean's face was contorted in a parody of handsomeness. His beautiful eyes and cheekbones blazed with the fire of his anger.

"Please, you are hurting me. Let go."

"Do you care that being denied my skin is a form of torture?"

What was he talking about? Ocean was accusing her of something she didn't understand, his grip on her arm painful enough to send a bolt of adrenaline through her.

"Let go of me. Now."

"How did you find out what I was? Who told you about my skin?"

Helena had been mentally rehearsing the moves from her self-defense class but at his words, she paused. "Ocean, listen to me, are you okay? Do you have pills you need to take or something?"

"You know what you did, you know what I am. It is too great a coincidence that you performed an ocean rite this morning and stole my skin the moment you stepped onto the boat."

"I didn't steal anything. Let go of my arm."

He released her. "My kind have been known to kill when their skin was finally returned."

Unbidden, a sound of fear escaped her lips.

"But then I look at you, and even now I can hear your heart beat, can feel your determination, your bravery and your fear. I have my skin. Why do I still feel enslaved by you?" His words were beautiful and sad, but spoken in angry tones.

"Ocean, Ocean, please explain what you are talking about. I don't understand. I don't want to hurt you."

"You already have." With that, he climbed the stairs out of the cabin.

Something was about to happen, Helena could feel it. She climbed the stairs only a few paces behind him. Ocean stood in the cockpit, near the rear railing.

"What—?" Helena bit back the rest of her questions when Ocean turned to her. He was beautiful under the summer moon. Powerful and wild, he was naked before her in the moonlight.

Turning his gaze from hers, Ocean slowly held up the blanket between his hands. The light breeze coming off the water made it look as if the blanket were moving all on its own.

Eyes now closed, Ocean brought the bare side of the fur to his chest, wrapping his arms around it and hugging it to his heart. Two steps had him through the little swinging door.

The words to call him back, to stop him, rose in her mind but she remained silent.

With one final glance at her, Ocean stepped off the back of the boat and tumbled into the night-blackened water.

"Ocean!" With a scream, she scrambled to the rear of the boat, kneeling on the small ledge, her knees slipping on the damp platform. "Ocean!" She scanned the surface of the water in vain. The night wind rippled the inky black water and the reflected moonlight illuminated the unbroken surface.

"Oh no, Ocean, where are you?" Helena forced herself to be still, forced herself to wait and watch. Over the thrumming of her heart, she heard water lapping against the hull, the muted canvas snap of the furled sails and the bark of seals.

It had been over two minutes. It was possible he was still under the water, able to hold his breath this long, but she was afraid for him.

Should she go in after him? Helena was a strong swimmer but had never been trained in search and rescue. She didn't know if she could get him out of the water if she found him. Helena moved to sit on the rear platform, her legs dangling over the side. Sucking in a breath as her bare thighs and bottom came into contract with the chilly ledge, Helena peered into the water.

A head popped out of the water. It was not a human head. Helena yelped and drew her feet up and back as the seal barked at her.

"Go away!" she shouted, not wanting the creature near the boat as she sat here waiting for Ocean. Then something else occurred to her. Maybe the seal had come to tell her Ocean was there, under the water, and needed her help. Weren't seals known for helping humans? Or was that dolphins?

Before she could decide if the seal's appearance meant she should jump in, it appeared directly under her dangling feet, its cold, wet nose and whiskers pressing into the sole of her right foot. With a yelp, Helena scrambled up, her frantic movements almost upsetting her balance and sending her down on top of the seal.

Back pressed against the railing, Helena fisted shaking hands, tears filling her eyes.

"Do I need to go in and look for him?" Curling her arms around her torso, she started to shake. "Why did he jump in the water? What does he think I stole? Why does he say I hurt him?" Tears slipped down her cheeks. "I love him."

The seal's head was still above the water and cocked to the side. Wiping her tears, Helena looked at the seal and slowly straightened. The seal was listening to her...understanding her?

"I must be losing my mind..." As if in a trance, Helena stepped to the edge once more. The seal tracked her movement.

"How...?"

The seal disappeared under the waves and propelled itself up onto the platform with Helena. Hands knotted in the T-shirt she wore, Helena pushed open the little door with her hip and backed into the main cockpit. The seal followed her, advancing across the deck with an odd rolling motion, its body large and ungainly out of the water.

When she stopped the seal did also.

Knowing she was insane, knowing it was madness and impossible and her grief and fear talking, Helena spoke to the seal.

"Ocean?"

The seal laid its head down on the deck and closed its eyes. In the next breath, the air around its long brown body shivered, and Helena's legs trembled as the aura tugged at her. She grabbed the back of the captain's chair as the pull increased, the feeling similar to standing knee-deep in the surf as a wave is drawn back to sea.

The seal's body was obscured by a thick blue mist, which hung for a moment and then started to dissipate, slipping away with the breeze, releasing what lay beneath.

Ocean lay still against the deck, his naked body speckled with water. He propped his upper body up on one elbow before lifting his head to look at Helena.

The sob she'd been holding in escaped. She stumbled toward him, falling to her knees at his side. Ocean knelt, letting her run trembling fingers over his face, chest and neck.

"Ocean, what are you?"

He cupped her face. "You really don't know?"

"No."

"Come on. It's time to explain."

Chapter Six

Ocean emerged from the bathroom where he'd hung the "blanket" to dry. Helena sat cross-legged on the bench, a mug of tea in her cold, trembling hands.

"Do you want anything else? Do you need more tea?" Ocean asked.

"No."

Ocean went into the tiny kitchenette and lifted his own cup, resting his towel-wrapped hips back against the counter, legs crossed at the ankle.

"You want answers."

"Please."

"Before I begin, let me ask you something. You truly had no idea what I was?"

Helena gripped her cup tighter as a flare of anger thawed her shock. "I told you already that I didn't."

"Fine. I'm sorry."

"Ocean, just tell me, what are you?"

"I'm a Selkie."

"Selkie?"

"One of the Sea Folk."

"Sea Folk?" Helena had reverted to answering questions with questions.

"The Sea Folk, the Sirens and the Selkie. Creatures who are half human, half animal."

"Wait, I feel like I know this." Helena struggled to recall an old memory, glad to have something to focus on besides the fact that she'd seen Ocean turn from seal to human.

"There are legends, most fiction rather than fact about the Selkie. You may have heard one."

"No, family history, and there were stories my grandmother used to tell. I—I can't remember what she said about Selkies, but I know I heard her speak of them, and the Sirens. She said they were known as the Sea Folk." If this was a coincidence it was an eerie one, but the other option, that their meeting was one of design or fate, was almost frightening.

"Gorgeous, what happened in the story?"

"My grandmother's grandmother disappeared. She had three children and when the youngest was six she disappeared, leaving her family behind. The youngest child, my grandmother's mother, said that her mother came back and visited her over the years, but only at times when her father was away. The rest of the family said she was imagining things, and when she talked of the sea people everyone said it was her imagination, her way of explaining why her mother abandoned her."

"She found her skin," Ocean said, providing the end of the story.

"Then it was true, my family story?"

"Yes, it sounds as if you are born of a Selkie."

Helena looked down into her cup, frowning as she reorganized her understanding in a manner that dealt with the fact that there was far more to the world than meets the eye. "You're not human."

"Yes and no. I have both human and seal bodies."

"The blanket?"

"Is my seal skin."

"Did I do something wrong when I touched it?"

"When you hid it—"

"I didn't hide it, all I did was put it away in the bench because I thought it was creepy that you had a dead animal blanket."

Ocean laughed ruefully. "And here I thought you were another sea creature, a Siren perhaps."

"Why would you think that?"

"This morning, when we were in the kayaks, you thanked the sun for rising. It is a blessing often used among the sea peoples."

"I did?"

"You did. Three times you lifted the water to the sky and let both water and sun kiss your face. It is powerful magic, old magic."

"Am I a Selkie? Like you?"

"You would know if you were. You would have been able to change from human to Selkie from the time you were a child. Even if you didn't know what you were, a longing for the water would have brought you to the ocean and you would have changed."

"But someone in my past was."

"Yes, it's in your blood."

"I had no idea" A terrible thought occurred to her. She had to look away, compose herself for a moment. "Is that why you had sex with me? Because you thought I was a Siren?"

"No. I had sex with you because you are gorgeous, but yes, I found you much more attractive once I saw you perform the blessing."

"Oh."

"Helena..."

"You didn't finish."

"Finish what?" he asked.

"What happened when I moved the skin?"

"When you took the skin it gave you power over me. The Selkies were a gift to the world, a gift that could be harnessed by humans, the skin a built-in weakness they could exploit, though it is hard on the Selkie. We crave the water and are only satisfied when we enter the water in seal form at least once a day. Without our skin we cannot change forms."

"It was only in the bench."

"I know, but I could have looked right at it, and as long you'd taken it from me and moved it, I would not have seen it."

"Then how do Selkies get their skin back?"

"There are two options for a Selkie to get his skin back. The first is to kill the person who took it. The other is to coax them into giving it to you, to try and pleasure them in whatever way is appropriate, so well that they would return it to you."

"So this has all been a lie." Heartsick, she set down her cup and rose, moving to the door and opening it so the cool night air flooded in.

"There is something else you should know."

"What else could there be?"

"I can read your mind."

At this she whirled, wide-eyed in shock. Ocean's face was serious.

"When? Why? How?"

"After the first time we had sex. Long ago a member of my family made a deal with a witch, if any of us were ever taken, we would be given the gift of sight into the mind of the one who held us prisoner, so we might always please them and be freed sooner."

"Everything between us has been a lie."

"No, everything has been the truth."

"But you only made love to me because you had no choice."

"It is true that I was compelled to obey you at times. There is magic in the skin which worked on both of us, magnifying what we felt."

She remembered the aggressive spike of arousal she'd felt when he first walked out of the bulkhead, right after she'd moved his skin.

"There is something in your blood that called to me, as I suspect something in me called to you," Ocean said, taking her in his arms.

"I just thought I wanted you because you're hot."

For the first time since changing, Ocean laughed in real amusement, holding Helena to his chest, both their bodies shaking with it.

"I can't believe I said that out loud."

Ocean kissed her neck. "You're awfully cute, gorgeous." He backed her up against the wall. The smile was back in his eyes as his lips descended on hers. The kiss was pure and long, lips fitting and molding together. When they broke the kiss, he rested his forehead on hers and it was so tender, tears slipped down Helena's face.

"I heard what you said when I was in my seal form," Ocean whispered against her cheek.

"The part where I said I love you?"

"Yes. And it made me very happy, because even as I tried to swim out to sea, I felt I was being called back to you. All day I've been drawn to you. I thought it was the skin, but I think that was only part of it."

Helena was shaking from the emotional impact of his words. Cradled in his arms, her tender heart supported by his loving embrace of her body, Helena was helpless to stop herself from falling a little more in love with him as he spoke.

"I love you." He went on. "You're kind, thoughtful, shy at times and exhibitionist at other, driven, successful and gorgeous. How could I not love you?"

"I love you," she repeated, wishing she had the beautiful speeches and perfect words to give him, but settling for a heartfelt confession.

Slipping her fingers into his hair, Helena kissed him, and with the kiss she told him she loved him and thanked him for loving her.

When he picked her up, Helena kissed any part of him she could reach. He laid her down on his bed and her sigh of pleasure turned into a gasp as he stripped the shirt off. Hands and lips set to work on her breasts and nipples.

When he thrust inside her it was perfect, and his strokes were long and slow so they didn't have to stop kissing. At her peak, when a cry of pleasure tore her mouth from his, Ocean held her, grounded her, and then she did the same for him as a few long strokes brought him to his completion, her hands stroking through his hair as he buried his head in her neck.

∞

It was nearing dawn before they stirred. They'd slept, tangled in each other, breathing each other's breath.

They kissed awake and then lay facing each other, still but for the occasional stroking of hair or soft touch of a finger to a lip.

Kissing Ocean's fingertip, Helena smiled. "I think I'm going to demand a refund."

He smiled in return. "I might just give it to you, though I do intend to drag you back into a kayak so we can explore the water together, but this time I won't be in the kayak with you. I'll accompany you as the seal."

"That would be amazing."

"There's something we need to take care of first."

"What?"

"Well, yesterday I would have spanked you because I could hear that you secretly wanted it and had fantasized about it. Since I can't read your mind any longer, I'm just going to spank you for being bad and stealing my skin."

As his grin grew wicked, Helena's eyes widened and with a yelp, she rolled off the bed. Ocean chased her, catching her, stealing a kiss and then releasing her. The chase led them out of the cabin and onto the deck.

When he caught her for the last time, there was no fear, only anticipation. He lifted her and stepped over the side, hurtling them both into the water. Safely wrapped in his arms, Helena knew she was home.

About the Author

Lila moved to Southern California where she obtained her degree in anthropology and currently resides in Hollywood, which provides an endless supply of exciting evenings and writing ideas. Having spent extensive time in France, Egypt and Turkey Lila speaks five languages, none of them (including English) fluently.

She has neither husband nor cats but there are some piranhas living in a fish tank behind her couch.

Visit her at www.liladubois.com.

Look for these titles by
Lila Dubois

Now Available:

Lights, Camera...Monsters

Printed in the United States
116646LV00004B/178-204/P